FRIES GRAVY DEATH

THE EB EATS DINER MYSTERIES
BOOK 1

POPPY BRIDGEMAN

Ebook ISBN: 978-1-990509-50-6
Paperback ISBN: 978-1-990509-51-3

Cover created by Getcovers

FREE BOOK

Use the QR code to Claim your copy of Burned by BLT
when you sign up for my newsletter learn how Eliza became
so determined to clear her name.

1

I gave the diner one last look before opening the doors for the day. Counters were wiped to a shine. Coffee was brewed strong and hot, sending its rich scent drifting through the air. Napkin dispensers were filled, salt and pepper shakers topped up, ketchup bottles wiped clean. EB Eats was ready.

The sign outside said EB Eats because "Eliza Burton's Place" felt like a huge mouthful. The full sign was also about four hundred dollars more than I wanted to spend when I ordered it, and simple had always suited me better anyway. I wasn't the fussy type. Never had been. I liked things straight-up and honest, whether it was coffee or conversation.

So far, my new life in Nueva Vida had gone surprisingly well. Six months in, and I still woke up some mornings half expecting it all to fall apart. Old habits. But here I was, standing in the middle of my very own diner, a place where I knew how many pounds of potatoes we went through in a week (a lot), and exactly how the light poured through the windows at seven-thirty in the morning (golden, warm, hopeful).

Luck? Maybe. Experience? Definitely. But I'd learned the hard way that the minute you start thinking you've got everything under control, life has a funny way of tripping you up. Chaos never needed an invitation to ooze through your door.

Six months ago, I was the prime suspect in my ex-husband's murder. That wasn't a chapter of my life I planned to relive any time soon. But I solved the case—long story—and cleared my name. When the dust settled, I was free and clear, and the half-a-million-dollar insurance payout I hadn't expected gave me the means to start over.

I sold my apartment in Oregon. Packed my things—Macchiato, my judgmental, long-haired, cat, included—and drove myself all the way to New Mexico. Nueva Vida. New life. It felt right.

Now I owned a cozy adobe house with a blue door that always made me smile, and a view of the mesas that turned purple at sunset. And EB Eats, my very own diner, where the air smelled like strong coffee and green chili most hours of the day.

I even had staff. Good people. That surprised me the most. Jacquie, my cook, would sleep in the kitchen if I let her. She was a wizard with a spatula and a drill sergeant about prep work. Lissa and Will, a brother and sister duo, handled the front. Lissa had charm for days and a memory for orders that bordered on supernatural. Will was quieter, always watching, but solid as they come. Anthone Sheret and Lola Adams did a bit of everything—bussing, prep, dishes, whatever needed doing. Anthone was still in his twenties and already had ideas about opening his own place one day. Lola was in her sixties, wrote romance novels, and insisted the diner was the best place in town to overhear dialogue.

I hate to be cliché, but these people were starting to feel like family.

And the customers? Some days it felt like I'd known them for years. Other days, I reminded myself I was still earning my place in this town. Nueva Vida was friendly, but like most small towns, it took time to truly belong.

I'd get there. If the locals had made one thing clear, it was this: No messing with the menu.

"No hipster food," Roy Martinez told me in my first week. "None of that fancy sous vide nonsense."

I promised I wouldn't change too much. Then I promptly added a weekly special. Three of them had stuck around because they were good, and nobody had complained. At least, not yet. A little creativity never hurt anyone.

Back in Oregon, my old boss had been obsessed with fusion food. Unfortunately, most of it tasted like the kitchen had gotten into a fight with itself and lost. He was a good cook with the palate of a colorblind interior designer.

We ran EB Eats from seven in the morning until eight at night, six days a week. The early hours belonged to truckers and ranchers. Tourists showed up mid-morning, wearing floppy hats and sunscreen, eager for something authentic. Locals drifted in all day long, looking for a reliable cup of coffee or something fried and familiar.

The smells of frying bacon and fresh tortillas hung in the air as Jacquie's voice floated out from the kitchen.

"They're waiting," she called. "Stop daydreaming and open the door before we have a riot on our hands."

Anthone was already ahead of me. He crossed the front of the diner in three long strides, flipped the sign to OPEN, and unlocked the door. He was quick, always eager. He had big plans, and I had no doubt he'd make them happen. I hoped he'd stick around long enough to teach someone else our ways when he did.

Bill Foster came in first, like clockwork. He headed for his usual stool at the counter, the one closest to the window where he could watch the world go by. His thermos thunked down next to him as he settled in with a satisfied grunt.

"You ought to open earlier," Bill said. "I could've used your corned beef hash an hour ago."

"If I open any earlier," I said, pouring his coffee, "I'll have to sleep here."

"Sounds cozy," he said, wrapping both hands around his mug. "Might save you rent."

"I like my own bed too much," I said with a grin. "And Macchiato would never forgive me."

Bill chuckled, shaking his head. "One day, I'm going to get that corned beef hash at two a.m. I look forward to it."

"You keep looking forward," I said, topping off his cup.

He winked. "That's what keeps me going."

I called his usual into the kitchen and turned to greet the next wave. The breakfast crowd was trickling in, familiar faces sliding into their usual booths, chatting quietly or reading the paper. The murmur of conversation, the hiss of the griddle, the soft clink of silverware on plates—it was its own kind of music.

For the first time in a long while, I wasn't running away from my life. I was running toward something. And I wouldn't have it any other way.

B y ten o'clock, the breakfast rush had simmered down to a gentle hum. A few stragglers lingered over their coffee, one pair of tourists sharing a plate of pancakes like they were splitting gold coins. Most mornings in Nueva Vida, the rush hit hard between seven-thirty and nine-thirty, then slowed to a manageable pace. That mid-morning lull was one of my favorite times in the diner.

The air smelled of maple syrup and bacon fat, the clatter from the kitchen softened, and the low murmur of conversation blended with the soft hum of the refrigerator. Even the sun seemed to pause as it slanted through the windows, warming the terracotta tiles and making the chrome gleam.

I was about to top off June Spenser's coffee when the door swung open hard enough to make the bell above it jangle like it had something to prove.

Alistair McKay.

He stood in the doorway for a second, letting his shadow fall across the room like some old Western villain who'd wandered in off the set. He had the build for it, too—broad shoulders, belly like a whiskey barrel, and a scowl carved so deep it probably had its own zip code.

He didn't say anything. Just scanned the room, his lips pinched tight, his gaze making a slow circuit around the booths and tables like he was taking attendance. Then, without a word, he spun on his heel and stormed out again, the door banging shut behind him.

I let out a breath I hadn't realized I was holding and shook my head.

"That one's wound tighter than a jackrabbit in a coyote den," June said, chuckling into her cup. Her silver hair caught the sunlight, making it gleam like polished pewter. She owned Outdoor Experiences, the tour office Jet worked for. She was a tight bundle of dry humor and cynicism.

"He ever smile?" I asked, refilling her coffee.

She gave me a look over her bifocals. "Not unless he's winning something."

"Well," I said, "he's certainly not winning friends."

"He's wondering why we're all here," June said, tilting her chin toward the scattering of customers. "Most of us still eat at his place. Can't do it every day, though. Man cooks like he's trying to clog every artery in town."

I stifled a laugh. "I've seen his menu. Everything comes with a side of gravy."

"And everything's deep-fried," she added. "Including, I think, the napkins."

I glanced toward the door, half expecting him to come back in, but the street outside was quiet again.

"I worry about him," I admitted. "He always looks like he's one argument away from a heart attack."

June made a sound somewhere between a snort and a giggle. "He's looked like that since he hit puberty. Don't waste your time worrying, honey. He'll outlive us all, just to spite us."

I smiled, but the knot in my stomach took its time unraveling. Alistair wasn't dangerous—probably—but there was something about his glare that made me double-check the locks at night.

"Can I help Jacquie?" Anthone's voice snapped me back to the present. He stood by the counter, a rag in one hand and his order pad in the other. He was eyeing the kitchen door like it was a chance to level up. "We're down to two booths of tourists and June here at the counter," he said. "I can cover out here too, if someone wants their check."

"You're eager," I said, nodding toward the back. "Go for it. I'll bus for a bit."

He didn't need telling twice. Anthone slipped through the swinging door with a little extra bounce in his step. I could already hear Jacquie giving him a hard time. She liked to claim she didn't want help in her kitchen, but I'd caught her smiling more than once when she was teaching him something new. She had a soft spot for hungry learners.

I grabbed the tub for dirty dishes and started clearing the last of the breakfast plates. The quiet was nice, but I knew it wouldn't last. Lunch wasn't far off, and lately, we'd had fewer and fewer of these slow stretches. It was great for business—but if service slipped, people noticed. That was the reality of running a diner in a town where word of mouth traveled faster than a jackrabbit with its tail on fire.

The bell over the door jingled again, and I glanced up. A man I didn't recognize stepped inside.

Short and broad through the chest, with a neck that disappeared into his shoulders. His dark suit was new enough to have a little shine but cheap enough to fool no one. His shoes were polished within an inch of their lives.

Sales rep, I guessed. Though for what, I couldn't say. We didn't get many business travelers in Nueva Vida. Our local festivals and weekend craft markets tended to draw tourists in cowboy boots and linen, not suits and ties.

He squinted around the room like he was sizing up the competition. "Do I seat myself?"

"Wherever you like," I said, giving him a polite smile and holding up the coffee pot. "Coffee to start?"

He scanned the counter stools, wrinkled his nose, then chose a booth by the front window—the only one still covered in dishes.

"Give me a second," I said, sweeping in with practiced efficiency. Plates stacked, napkins gathered, crumbs wiped away with a clean rag.

He slid into the booth before I finished, leaning away like he was afraid I might accidentally drop a half-eaten pancake in his lap.

I placed a fresh cup and saucer in front of him, along with a rolled set of cutlery. "Here's a menu," I said, offering it with a little more cheer than I felt. "Our special today is Southwest poutine. Hand-cut fries topped with chili gravy and cheese. You can get it red, green, or Christmas."

He picked up the menu and glanced at it like it was written in another language. "What's Christmas?" he asked, his voice nasal and flat.

"Red and green chili gravy," I explained. "It's the best of both worlds."

He looked me over then, slow and deliberate, like he was calculating whether I had any idea what I was talking about.

"Special," he said at last. "Christmas style. Water, no ice. And coffee. Keep the refills coming."

I nodded, pouring his water and pointing out the cream and sugar. "Be right back with your order."

He didn't thank me. I wasn't surprised.

Lissa came up beside me as I rang in his ticket. She leaned in close. "I don't like the way he looked at you," she whispered.

"I've seen worse," I said. "He's probably just hungry."

"I don't think that's it," she said. "You want me to ask Anthone to come back out?"

I considered it but waved her off. "We can handle it. We're pros."

Lissa didn't look convinced, but she let it go.

Jacquie rang the bell a few minutes later, calling out the order with her usual no-nonsense snap. Before I could grab the plate, Lissa was there, adding a careful sprinkle of cilantro and crushed red chili to finish it off.

"He's still staring at the window," she said.

"Maybe he's meditating," I offered.

"Maybe he's casing the place," she muttered.

He didn't say anything when Lissa set the plate down. Just picked up his fork and started eating like it was a chore.

I took a payment from one of our regulars and handed them their receipt, laughing at a joke I'd already forgotten by the time I turned back. When I glanced at the window booth again, the man was pushing his empty bowl away.

I walked over, wiping my hands on my apron. "Did you enjoy it?" I asked.

"It was okay," he said. "Not poutine." He said it like the word tasted bad. "I've had real poutine in Quebec," he went on. "Can't stand it when people slap a fancy name on something and think they can charge more."

He stabbed a finger at the menu on the table. "It's fries and gravy with cheese and chilies. Not even the right kind of cheese."

If he hated it so much, I wasn't sure why he'd cleaned the bowl.

"I agree," I said, keeping my tone even. "It's tough to get cheese curds this far south. I do the best I can."

He sniffed. "Not a good excuse. I'll be reviewing you." He met my eyes then, a little gleam of satisfaction in his. "I don't play games."

Oh, buddy, you have no idea. But I didn't say that. "I'm sorry we didn't meet your expectations," I said instead.

People like him didn't want an argument. They wanted a target. I wasn't giving him one.

"Check," he said shortly.

I dropped it off with a nod and walked away, keeping my smile in place until I turned my back.

Lissa sidled up again. "Just having a bad day?"

"Don't make me laugh," I murmured, stifling a grin. "He'll think it's about him."

"It is," she said, and I had to bite my lip.

Anthone came out to clear the table once the man had paid. He dropped the bills off at the counter and raised an eyebrow. "Two-dollar tip," he said. "Classy."

"Good thing I pay you a living wage," I said. I rang up the sale, dropped the two bucks in the tip jar, and glanced out the window in time to see the man disappear down the street.

I shook off the uneasy feeling that lingered in his wake.

Lunch was coming. There were customers to feed. And a lot of coffee yet to pour.

3

———

The bell above the door jingled again, followed by a rush of desert air that smelled faintly of sage and warm earth.

Jet Rivers stepped inside, grinning like he didn't have a care in the world.

I swear, the man had a personal spotlight. Tall and lean, with dark hair that always looked like he'd just run a hand through it, Jet had the kind of green eyes that made people sit up and pay attention. He was tanned from long days in the sun, guiding tourists up climbing routes or leading horseback rides along dusty trails.

He crossed the diner with an easy stride and rested his arms on the counter like he belonged there—which, by now, he did. "That guy who just left?" he said, tipping his chin toward the street. "Bit of a jerk."

"You noticed," I said, wiping my hands on my apron as I came over. "He wasn't exactly subtle."

Jacquie's voice drifted from the kitchen. "Order for Jet—two minutes!"

She was always on top of it. Even when she complained, she liked making sure the regulars were taken care of.

Jet gave me a look. "He give you a hard time?"

"Only about the cheese," I said. "And the fact that I had the audacity to call fries with chili gravy 'poutine.' He was deeply offended."

Jet chuckled. "They're always so passionate about the cheese."

I grinned. "A man needs a cause."

He shook his head, then sobered. "He shoved past Mrs. Waverly on the sidewalk. Almost knocked her over."

I stilled, the rag in my hands forgotten. "What?"

"She's fine," he said quickly. "Told me herself. Said the day she couldn't handle a rude man was the day she'd lie down in her coffin."

I let out a breath, then chuckled despite myself. "That sounds like her."

Mrs. Waverly was a fixture in town, the sort of woman who wore orthopedic shoes and carried a purse big enough to double as a weapon. Ninety-two, if the rumors were true, and as sharp as they came.

"She's tougher than most," Jet agreed. "But still. Guy like that? No manners."

I leaned a hip against the counter. "You know what they say about opinions and butts."

He laughed, his grin crinkling the corners of his eyes. "Everyone's got one."

Jacquie hit the bell then, and I grabbed the brown paper bag she set on the pass. It smelled like roasted green chili and something fried—Jacquie's signature chicken burger.

"You two picnicking in the back of the bookstore again?" I asked, handing the bag over.

"Kashvi's idea," he said, taking it. "We're reorganizing the history section today. Lunch and labor."

"Sounds romantic."

He gave me a wry smile. "You try telling her that."

I shook my head. "No thanks. She scares me more than you do."

Truth was, Kashvi Verma was one of my closest friends in Nueva Vida, even if she pretended she didn't believe in close friends. Her bookstore, The Open Page, was the coziest place in town, next to EB Eats. Jet had been sweet on her for months now. They were a couple with no commitments—her choice. He never pushed for more. Just showed up when she needed a hand. I wasn't sure if she'd ever give in, but if anyone could wait her out, it was Jet.

"I'll swing by after work," I said. "If you two have time for a night of cards."

"Bring your A-game," he said. "I plan to win."

"You always plan to win," I called as he left, the door swinging shut behind him.

I took a deep breath, letting the rhythm of the diner settle in around me again. The scent of coffee brewing. The scrape of forks on plates. The muted conversations, broken by the occasional burst of laughter. The sound of home, if I was being honest with myself.

I grabbed the tub of fresh condiments and started making my way around the booths, checking ketchup bottles, wiping surfaces. Lissa and Anthone were clearing tables and chatting with customers, and Jacquie was already deep in prep for the lunch rush.

In about an hour, the afternoon crew would start filtering in. Will would take over from Lissa at the front, and Lola would start bussing, though she was just as likely to linger at a table, chatting and collecting new material for her romances.

We all wore more than one hat around here. No one cared about job titles as long as the coffee was hot and the food was good.

Will was Lissa's stepbrother. She'd asked me to give him a shot when she came on board. Said he was trying to leave his old life behind. My first impression when he sat through the interview? He was rough around the edges, sure, but I'd seen something solid underneath all that wariness. So I gave him a week's probation, and he hadn't let me down.

Lola was a whole different story. She was in her sixties, wore her long gray hair in a braid down her back, and had a laugh that could shake the walls. She said bussing tables kept her from turning into a cranky old lady. I wasn't about to argue. She kept her notebook in her apron pocket and scribbled ideas for characters between clearing plates. She claimed no one ever recognized themselves in her books, but I wasn't convinced.

"You want to eat before the rush?" Jacquie called, poking her head out of the kitchen. "I already had mine."

My stomach rumbled in response.

"Just a quick bite," I said, making my way to the little table we kept by the back door for breaks.

Jacquie handed me a plate with half a green chili quesadilla and a small salad on the side.

"I added bacon," she said.

"You're a saint," I told her.

She snorted. "Eat fast."

I did. And as I ate, I watched the sunlight slant through the windows, catching the glint of chrome on the counter stools. The steady rhythm of the place soothed me. This was mine. I'd worked hard for it. And I wasn't about to let anything mess it up.

4

The day drifted along in that steady, comforting rhythm I was starting to think of as my new normal. The occasional clatter of dishes, the low sizzle of something delicious coming off Jacquie's grill. Every now and then, the door chimed and someone familiar —or not—stepped inside.

By late afternoon, the regulars were outnumbering the tourists again. The light had shifted to that honeyed glow that made the polished counter gleam and set the chrome napkin holders winking at me like they knew something I didn't.

I was wiping down the booths near the window when I noticed Will stiffen behind the counter. His gaze locked on someone coming through the door, and he tensed like a guitar string pulled too tight.

Cassidey.

I'd met her once before, though "met" was probably generous. She was one of Will's old crew—back from the days when he was making bad decisions with worse company. Skinny as a fence post and pale in a way that had nothing to do with her natural coloring, she shuffled in like she hadn't eaten in days. The second Will spotted her, he was moving fast, intercepting her halfway to the counter.

"You don't own the world," she told him before he even spoke. Her voice was flat but defiant. "I'm not here for trouble. Just hungry."

She shifted her weight from foot to foot, a little sway that made me think she wasn't sure whether to stand her ground or bolt.

I walked over slowly, wiping my hands on my apron.

"You're welcome to sit," I said. "You bring trouble, you're out. But if you sit quiet and eat, like I said, you're welcome."

Her chin lifted a fraction. "I won't bring no trouble," she said.

Will muttered something under his breath that sounded a lot like "we'll see," but he stepped back.

I caught Jacquie's eye through the pass window. "Double her fries," I said.

Jacquie nodded and went back to the grill.

Will lingered nearby, his arms crossed tight over his chest. "You made it clear," he said quietly, "first couple weeks I was here. No gang stuff. No attitude."

"And you've stuck to that," I said. "Now it's her turn to try."

He gave me a look that held more doubt than hope, but he didn't argue. "She's not strong enough," he said. "They'll pull her back in."

"Maybe," I said. "Maybe not. But if she's hungry and we can feed her, I'm not going to turn her away."

It wasn't that I was naive. I'd lived through enough to know better. But I also knew what it felt like to be desperate and overlooked. And more than that, I knew people could surprise you.

Cassidey sat by the window, hunching low in her seat like she was waiting for someone to throw her out anyway.

Lissa brought her a glass of water and set it down without a word. Small kindnesses, I'd learned, went further than people expected.

The rest of the afternoon passed like any other. Regulars drifted in for late lunches or a coffee break. Tourists wandered through, snapped a few photos, and asked about the specials.

No one marched in behind Cassidey with a crew of thugs. No one flipped a table or tried to rob us. Dinner came and went, steady and smooth. We sold out of the Southwest poutine around seven, which made me think it was time to consider adding it to the regular menu—despite what the Quebec purists might have to say.

By closing, the dining area was spotless. I sent everyone home, even Jacquie, who insisted on arguing about it until I threatened to lock her out. The truth was, I liked closing the diner by myself. It gave me time to breathe, to take in the quiet, to appreciate what I was building here. Wiping down the tables, sweeping and mopping the floors until they gleamed, sanitizing the counters so they smelled faintly of pine and lemon. I had a system. I liked my system. It made me feel in control. And after the last few months of building stability in a new place, I wasn't about to mess with what worked.

I was finishing up the kitchen, wiping down the last of the prep surfaces and humming quietly to myself, when I heard the knock.

It came from the front window. My heart did a little stutter step. I set down the rag carefully and walked toward the door, drying my hands on my apron. For one brief, ridiculous second, I thought maybe it was Will's prediction coming true—Cassidey's gang back to make trouble.

But when I reached the front, I saw a man and woman standing outside. He had one hand shading his eyes and the other holding up a badge. Cops. And just like that, my stomach dropped.

I cracked open the door but didn't budge from behind it. "You'll need to introduce yourselves," I said. I wasn't about to let strangers in, badge or not, without knowing who I was dealing with.

"Detective George Kramer," the man said. He looked tired, like he'd missed a few too many nights of sleep. Rumpled suit, five o'clock shadow, and the kind of blue eyes that probably used to be bright but now just looked weary. "And this is Detective Denise Collett."

Collett was taller, younger, sharper. Hair in a short natural afro, dressed like she was about to walk into a board meeting. She gave me a nod, but there was no smile in it.

"Can we come in?" Kramer asked. "I doubt you want to have this conversation on the sidewalk."

I hesitated. The diner was clean for the night. I wasn't going to spoil that by serving food, or coffee to cops I didn't know, but I wasn't rude.

"Come in," I said, pushing the door open wider. "I just finished cleaning, so don't get comfortable."

They slid into the first booth near the door. I stayed standing. It wasn't petty. Okay, maybe it was a little petty. But after what I'd been through six months ago, I wasn't in the mood to make life easy for any detective. Even if he did have tired eyes and a polite tone.

"We're investigating a murder," Kramer said without preamble. He pulled out his phone and tapped to bring up a photo. "Do you know this man?"

I glanced at the screen. It was the poutine guy. He was lying on his back, eyes staring, his mouth open like he'd been about to complain one last time. The alley pavement under his head was stained dark.

I took a steadying breath. "You could have mentioned he was dead before you showed me the picture."

"We said it was a murder investigation," Collett said. She sounded annoyed, like I'd asked a stupid question.

Kramer gave her a sharp look and turned back to me. "I'm sorry. But we need to know. Did you recognize him?"

I kept my hands loose at my sides. "He was in here earlier today. Had the special. Complained about the cheese. Left a lousy tip." I met Kramer's gaze. "How did he die? Not from my cooking, I hope."

The corner of his mouth twitched. "It wasn't poison. You're not a suspect."

Collett didn't look convinced.

Kramer continued, "He had a receipt from your place. We're trying to track his movements."

I nodded slowly. "I heard he was rude to Mrs. Waverly when he left here. Maybe she finally had enough."

Kramer's mouth quirked. "We'll check into that."

Collett scribbled something in her notebook. "Do you know the name Peter Trent?"

I went still.

I did know that name. My ex-husband Joseph had mentioned him a few times, back when his business dealings had started to go south—taking his moral compass right along with them.

"The name does ring a bell. Maybe it's a different Peter Trent," I said. "The one I'm thinking about was a friend of my ex-husband, Joseph Carr."

"Your husband's contact information?" Collett said, holding her pen ready to record my answer.

"My ex-husband," I emphasized his status. "He died."

"When did your ex-husband pass?" Kramer asked.

"Six months ago," I said quietly. "Murdered."

Collett looked up from her notebook. "That's two men connected to you who are dead." Her tone was sharp enough to cut.

Kramer stood and gestured for Collett to do the same. "Thank you for your time," he said.

I stayed put. "Am I a suspect now? You said I wasn't."

"We'll be in touch," Kramer said. "And no, you're not a suspect. But we'll need to follow up on your ex-husband's case."

"Fine," I said. "I'm not going anywhere."

"Good," he said. "Unless Mrs. Waverly confesses. Then maybe we'll all get lucky and we can close this case fast."

His faint grin didn't make me feel any better.

I locked the door after them, then stood for a long moment staring at the empty diner. Déjà vu was an ugly feeling.

And I had the distinct sense I was about to live through it all over again.

5

I wiped down the last booth at EB Eats again, watching the suds glisten for a moment before I ran a dry towel over the vinyl. I checked the front and back doors twice, maybe three times, then slipped off my apron and grabbed the takeout bag waiting for me by the door.

Nueva Vida had settled into a soft hush by the time I locked up. The pastel sunset was melting into velvety dusk, the streetlamps flickering on with a faint buzz. Over at The Open Page, golden light spilled through the old-fashioned windows. It was one of those rare places that still had hand-painted lettering on the glass and a bell that jingled when you walked in. It made you feel like you were stepping into a storybook.

Kashvi and Jet were already waiting inside. Well, Kashvi was waiting, I could see her checking something at the cash desk. Jet was usually a beat ahead of the rest of us when it came to settling in for a party.

Kashvi's story reminded me of my own in more ways than one. She'd left behind family, expectations, and judgment when she moved to Nueva Vida. Five years ago, she'd bought The Open Page on a whim and met Jet somewhere along the way. She told me once, when we were both holding a battered copy of *The Alchemist*, that even if she changed her mind about being single—which she hadn't—her family wouldn't approve of Jet. I'd only nodded. Their life was their life. After my own marriage crash-and-burned, I wasn't exactly penciling in a second round, either.

I gripped the bag in one hand and rapped lightly on the glass before Kashvi appeared and waved me in. She was a tiny thing, maybe five foot two if she was wearing heels, and always buzzing with energy. Tonight, her pixie cut was dyed a brilliant blue, and the violet contacts she liked to wear turned her dark brown eyes into something magical. If Nueva Vida had fairies, Kashvi could easily be their queen.

"Go on back," she said, clicking the lock behind me. "Jet's already opened the first beer."

The back room wasn't fancy, but it was cozy in that over-stuffed kind of way. Books stacked in boxes or half-sorted piles on three walls, like they were waiting for their next reader. A folding table doubled as a desk, with three metal chairs pushed around it. A little string of fairy lights blinked above the doorway to the washroom, giving the space a faint glow that softened the edges.

Jet looked up from where he was flipping through a dog-eared mystery novel. His dark hair a little messy, and his smile lit up his face. He always seemed to be somewhere between relaxed dude and active outdoors expert.

"Did you hear?" he asked before I'd even put the food down.

"Hold on," Kashvi cut in, taking the bag from me. "We eat first. Then we can talk about whatever drama's got your hackles up."

"Fair enough," Jet said, raising his bottle in salute.

I pulled out the containers—vegetable curry, rice, butter chicken, not from the diner—and handed Kashvi a warm naan fresh from the tandoor. The spicy, savory aroma filled the room, wrapping around us like a blanket. It was the kind of meal you ate with your hands and your heart. Despite Jet's usual war on carbs, he took a scoop of rice and chicken without protest, though he focused more on sipping his Kingfisher.

I tore off a piece of naan and used it to scoop up a bite, ignoring the spoon resting politely at my place. There was something about sharing food this way that made it feel less like dinner and more like family.

"All right," I said after I'd finished chewing. "Heard what?"

Jet leaned back in his chair. "That guy—the one who trashed your poutine and nearly knocked over Mrs. Waverly? He's dead."

I paused mid-scoop. "I know."

Kashvi set down her beer with a thunk. "Wait until I'm done eating before we get to the details. You know the rules."

"Sorry." Jet gave her an apologetic smile, but his eyes were still on me.

I finished my bite, letting the warmth of the curry settle in my belly before I spoke. "The cops already stopped by the diner. They made a point of saying it wasn't my food." I tried unsuccessfully for a smile that didn't feel tight. "But I wouldn't mind knowing the official story before I get cornered at the farmer's market tomorrow."

"Stabbing," Jet said, keeping his voice low. "Multiple wounds. I heard it from a friend at the medical examiner's office, but she had to cut the call short when her boss walked in."

Kashvi blew out a breath. "At least it wasn't poisoning." She gave me a pointed look. "Not that we ever doubted you."

"Yeah, thanks," I said, though my stomach tightened. "They came by because he had the receipt from the diner in his pocket. His name was Peter Trent." I swirled the last of my beer around in the bottle, watching the bubbles pop and disappear. "He knew Joseph. My ex-husband."

Neither of them said anything for a moment. Just the soft sounds of chewing and the faint hum of traffic outside the window.

"I haven't told you everything about Oregon," I added. "But it's going to come out. Once the press gets wind of my name, they'll connect the dots."

"We're not going to let this blow up on you," Kashvi said firmly, wiping her fingers on a paper napkin. "You're not that person. And people here know you."

"Some of them," Jet said. "But word's already spreading. Nothing specific. Just whispers."

I met his gaze. "I can handle whispers. I've had practice."

"You sure?" Kashvi's voice softened. "Because if you need backup—"

"You two are already my backup." I forced a small grin. "Besides, I pointed the cops to Mrs. Waverly. If anyone's capable of knocking a guy off his feet—and maybe stabbing him for good measure—it's her."

Kashvi snorted. "She'd need an accomplice. Her knees are shot."

The laughter felt good. It took the edge off the worry gnawing at me.

"But seriously," Kashvi went on, "you don't think Alistair will use this to come after you?"

I sighed, leaning back. "He's all bluster." I hoped. If

people started to believe I was dangerous, Alistair's long game of running me out of town might just work.

"Who talked to you?" Jet asked.

"Detectives George Kramer and Denise Collett. She's... eager."

Jet and Kashvi exchanged a look. It made me sit up a little straighter. "What?" I asked. "Do I need to worry?"

"She's new," Kashvi said. "Trying to prove herself. George is solid, though. Grew up here until his parents moved—he must have been eight or nine at the time. Most people forgot that and label him as a big city guy."

That seemed totally unfair.

"He's also cute," Kashvi added, raising an eyebrow at me. "And single."

"Oh no," I said, mock glaring at her. "Don't you start matchmaking."

"I'm just saying." She winked. "You could do worse."

"If he's smart, he'll find someone else to focus on," I muttered. "Otherwise, I'll have to clear my name—again."

Jet tipped his bottle toward me. "Then we'll help you."

I clinked mine against his and Kashvi's. "To having a team."

Outside, the wind rattled the windowpanes softly, but inside the bookstore, surrounded by curry-scented air, old books, and two people who had my back, I felt like maybe—just maybe—I could weather this storm.

6

"I can see why you'd be nervous," Jet said, his voice calm, steadying. He leaned forward, resting his elbows on his knees. "By morning, Alistair will have researched your history. George too, and he can talk to the cop on that case. Alistair will just use the tidbits to fuel his imaginary slights."

He took a sip of beer, then added, "But there's not much you can do tonight. I can recommend a lawyer if it comes to that."

I frowned. A lawyer? If I needed one, it was already too late. My lawyer back in Oregon had been amazing, but her job hadn't been to clear my name before I was charged. She hadn't been able to stop the accusations from hanging around my neck like a cinder block. This time, I had to keep the stain off my reputation before it stuck. Back then, I'd known the players. I'd had a list of names and questions. That had been my turf.

Nueva Vida wasn't my turf. Not yet.

Sure, I had regulars who knew my name, my diner, and maybe even my go-to pie recipe. But I wasn't part of the deep roots here. Not like Kashvi and Jet were. Not like Alistair was. And now, there were people depending on me. If EB Eats closed down even for a few days, my crew would be hurting. I couldn't let that happen.

"I'm going to find the killer," I said, more confident than I felt. The words hung in the air like steam off a hot cup of coffee. For a second, pride flickered inside me. Then the cold rush of questions flooded in. What did I even know about the man? Who would want him dead? Where did I start?

"I can't let people start asking questions about me," I added. "Not again."

Kashvi stacked our plates with neat efficiency, sliding cutlery into a bright red plastic bowl she kept under the table for clean-up nights like this. She glanced at me over her shoulder. "How?" she asked, keeping her tone gentle.

I watched her move while I came up with an answer. Even in the dim glow of the fairy lights, she was all energy and precision. Her bangles clinked softly as she worked. "I know people aren't thrilled George and Denise got promoted over some of the local cops," she said, "but there's a reason they did. They're good. You don't have to take this on yourself."

"I did it before," I said. My voice was quieter now, but steady. "I just need to know who to talk to. And you two know everyone."

Jet rubbed the back of his neck, thinking hard. "Gossip," he said. "This town runs on it. You'll need to find out who talked to Trent while he was here—besides you. Any clue why he came to Nueva Vida in the first place? Why someone might've wanted him dead?"

I chewed my bottom lip. "I wondered about that when I first saw him. He wasn't dressed like a tourist." I thought back to his cheap suit and expensive-looking watch, all wrong for a casual dinner at a small-town diner. "And we don't exactly have conference centers nearby."

Jet tipped his head, considering. "What do you remember about his relationship with Joseph?" he asked. "Maybe there's a clue there. Something about what he did?"

I had been ready to defend myself. To explain why I couldn't sit back and let the police handle it. Why this wasn't something I could walk away from. But the words died on my lips.

"You're not going to try to talk me out of it?" I asked, surprised. Bewildered, really. I'd expected protests. Instead, they were... onboard?

Kashvi gave me a look. "It's dangerous," she said plainly. "This isn't shoplifting. Someone killed him. And this is a small town. There are secrets here people don't want uncovered—old ones."

"You could get into trouble with the cops," Jet added. "They won't like you poking around their case."

"Oh, and Detective Collett will be thrilled if you solve this before she does," Kashvi added, arching a brow. "Stealing her chance at glory? Yeah. Great way to make a lifelong enemy."

They both stared at me for a long beat, and then they laughed. I couldn't help it—I laughed too. It was warm and familiar, like the chai Kashvi sometimes made on cold mornings, spicy and sweet.

"It'll ruin your chances with George," Jet said with a grin.

I rolled my eyes. "Not interested in dating."

"You say that," Kashvi said in a sing-song voice.

"I say it because it's true." I stood and gathered the dishes. "Let me wash these."

I took the bowl of plates and utensils into the little wash-room. The sink was tiny but did the job. Warm water ran over my hands as I scrubbed. Kashvi's hand soap smelled like lavender and lemon—comforting, in a way I hadn't expected. I rinsed the plates and left them to dry on the little rack by the window.

When I came back, Kashvi had produced three small notepads with floral covers and matching pens that looked like they smelled like strawberries.

"If we're serious about this," Jet said, "we need to get to know the victim. Research Trent, figure out who he was meeting here. What he was involved in."

"Maybe why he was such a pain in the butt," Kashvi added.

"And why he was here," Jet finished. "That's a big one."

Kashvi placed the notebooks in front of us like we were planning a heist. "We need to brainstorm."

I held up a hand. "Slow down. All those things you said about why I shouldn't get involved? They apply to both of you."

"We're your friends," Jet said simply. "How do you expect us to sit back and watch you deal with this alone?"

Kashvi smiled softly, sliding a sticky note pad out of her pocket. "Life's a risk," she said. "But you're not taking it solo."

They meant it. I knew they did. The thought squeezed my chest in a way I wasn't used to. This was what friendship looked like, in Nueva Vida anyway. And I wasn't about to take it for granted.

"Okay," I said. "Actions. We need to learn about Trent. Who he talked to. Who he contacted. Maybe figure out what he and Joseph were doing before... before everything. I don't think it was money laundering. But if it was—does Nueva Vida even have a criminal underworld?"

"Good question," Kashvi said. "You could ask Will."

I shook my head. "Not pulling Will back into his old life."

She didn't push. Just nodded.

"Who can you call from back home?" Jet asked. "To find out if Trent brought old problems with him?"

I thought about it. Finley, the detective back in Oregon, probably wouldn't tell me anything she hadn't before. But Billy—Joseph's assistant—might know something. He'd always liked me. No one else came to mind.

"I'll make a call," I said. "But I want more information first. Details. Real questions."

"Social media," Kashvi said. "He might have posted where he's staying."

"I'm not optimistic," I said. "He's older, probably doesn't live his life online. And if he was hiding, he definitely wouldn't post his whereabouts."

"We need a hacker," Jet said, laughing. "All the good shows have hackers."

I chuckled. "Know any?"

Jet and Kashvi both shook their heads.

"Didn't think so," I said. "We'll start with social media. Maybe we'll get lucky."

"I'll bring my laptop," Kashvi said. "We won't know until we try, Eliza."

As they scribbled notes and brainstormed, I made a quiet promise to myself. I'd do everything I could to keep them safe. I was grateful they had my back—but I wasn't going to let them get hurt. Not on my account.

And with that, we began.

7

K ashvi's office was a lot more versatile than it looked. Function over form, with just enough personality to make it inviting. She'd set it up that way, even if it hadn't quite followed the original plan.

The boxes of books were neatly stacked against one wall, each one labeled in Kashvi's looping handwriting. The table in the middle of the room was plain but sturdy, just big enough for us to crowd around—whether it was to brainstorm over dinner, balance ledgers, or tonight—dive into amateur sleuthing.

Kashvi had told me once, back when we first met, that she'd dreamed of this space being a cozy hub for the town. A quiet spot for writers' groups to gather, or book clubs that had outgrown someone's living room. A study room for students during finals. Maybe even a pop-up yoga class if the weather turned bad.

But then the first order of books for The Open Page arrived. She hadn't had the shelf space to display them all, and the room became a catch-all for overflow, business paperwork... and, as it turned out, our little detective agency.

The front of the store had its own energy. A circle of cushy, mismatched armchairs gathered under the wide windows, where regulars hung out to sip Kashvi's spiced tea and borrow her Wi-Fi. It was like a miniature version of the library, only with better lighting and the faint smell of vanilla candles.

But back here? This was our war room.

Kashvi set up her old but reliable laptop on the table, scooting her chair close so Jet and I could lean in on either side. The soft click of her typing was the only sound for a few moments, until she said, "Shall I start with a Google search on his name?"

"It's probably a pretty common name," I said. "But maybe it'll show where he's got profiles."

She hit enter, and we stared at the screen. The first few results were all about a politician from Quebec. Not our Peter. Rather than wasting time, Kashvi immediately started refining the search. She tried his name with 'lawyer' tacked on, even though I wasn't sure that was how he'd connected with Joseph. Then she added New Mexico, Oregon, and Joseph Carr to the mix.

No luck. Just dead ends and spammy links. It was like trying to find a specific grain of sand at the bottom of the arroyo.

"That hacker would be handy right about now," Jet muttered, leaning back in his chair with a frustrated huff.

Kashvi clicked open another tab. "If we're going to hand anything over to Kramer and Collett, it needs to be clean. No hacking. No gray areas."

She was right, of course. If we found the killer but used

anything shady to do it, the case would unravel, and we'd end up in the hot seat instead.

And none of us knew a hacker anyway.

"Try more specific," I suggested. "Search Nueva Vida. Maybe the diner name. Maybe he managed to leave a review before..." Before he died. I let the sentence trail off, feeling the weight of it.

Kashvi's fingers danced over the keyboard, searching in two different tabs at once. She was fast. Focused. "No review," she said after a beat. "Probably a good thing. One-star reviews from murder victims aren't the kind of press you want."

I gave her a dry look, but she was already focused on the second tab. Then she straightened. "Wait. Here he is."

Jet and I both leaned in as three social media accounts popped up—Facebook, Instagram, and LinkedIn. Kashvi opened each one in a new window, her bangles clinking softly as she moved. Several Peter Trents on each one.

"Let's split them up," Jet said. "Eliza and I can use our phones, make notes. It'll be faster."

It was already late, and I had to be up at four a.m. so I could open the diner for the breakfast crowd. "I'll take LinkedIn," I offered. I still had my old business account, which made navigating profiles a little easier.

The room fell quiet, except for the occasional scratch of pen on paper or the gentle hum of the laptop fan. Outside, I could hear the muffled sounds of tires on pavement as someone drove by. Inside, the glow of the fairy lights softened the shadows, giving the room a quiet intimacy.

"Found him on Facebook," Kashvi said after a while. "Profile's still active. I followed him."

"Unfollow," I said sharply. "Right now. We don't want

your name showing up. Or the killer's curiosity getting piqued."

"Relax," Kashvi said, not taking her eyes off the screen. "I used the bookstore account. It'll just look like local businesses following potential customers. No one's going to think twice."

I hoped she was right.

"We can't avoid risks," Jet said, glancing at me. "We'll be careful. But we have to know what's out there."

I sighed. I remembered telling myself something similar back in Oregon, when I'd convinced myself I could outsmart a murderer. And yeah, I'd survived. Barely. But I still carried the scars—some you could see, some you couldn't.

"We know the danger," Kashvi said, glancing at me over the rim of her glasses. "The plan is still to turn over everything to Kramer when we have enough to help. That hasn't changed."

I hesitated. There were a hundred arguments in my head, and none of them sounded convincing. They were determined. Maybe more determined than I was, at this point. "But—" I started.

"But nothing," Jet cut in, his voice gentle but firm. "This isn't just about you anymore. This murder affects all of us. Even if it's just gossip, it threatens you, the diner, and the whole community."

I blew out a breath. "I'm not going to let either of you get hurt."

Kashvi just smiled, like she already knew I'd say that. "We're okay right now," she said. "We're careful. We're in this together."

And I was pretty sure if I shut it down, they'd go behind my back. So I nodded. For now.

Kashvi's phone buzzed, and she checked it. Her expression tightened, and she tapped out a reply before looking up. "Alistair," she said. "Fishing for details. I told him to stop asking."

"So we were right," Jet said. "If he's reaching out to you, I'm sure he's already been in contact with half the town."

That confirmed what I'd already suspected. Alistair was stirring the pot, and soon everyone in Nueva Vida would be wondering what role I played in Peter Trent's death.

"Five more minutes," Kashvi said, glancing at the clock. "I don't want to fall into a rabbit hole. If he's got a TikTok, we're doomed. I'll be watching investment videos until sunrise."

I smiled, but it didn't feel like one that quite reached my eyes. "I've got a few things," I said, jotting notes in my pad. Questions mostly. Clues would come later.

"Me too," Jet said. "Maybe useful. We'll see."

Kashvi stretched, cracking her knuckles. "All right. Just the highlights, and then sleep. Let our subconscious work on the puzzle overnight."

We went over what we had so far: Peter Trent's profiles painted a picture of a man who floated from place to place. His LinkedIn said he was an independent financial adviser. The kind who promised sky-high returns on low-risk investments—too good to be true, if you asked me. His social media was all glossy graphs and vague posts about opportunities on the horizon. Very little personal interaction. Almost no comments.

"A starting point," Jet said, closing his notebook with a snap. "Tomorrow, we dig deeper."

"And maybe we'll find something on Reddit," Kashvi added, grabbing her jacket. "People love to overshare there."

Jet stood up and stretched, then turned to us with a grin. "I'm walking you both home."

"You don't have to," I said, but I was already gathering my things.

"Maybe not," he said. "But this is Nueva Vida. And that's what we do."

And as we stepped out into the cool night, the stars bright overhead and the sleepy hush of the town wrapping around us, I realized something: no matter what came next, I wasn't doing this alone.

8

The next morning, I opened EB Eats to a line waiting at the door. Not unusual on a Friday, but today there was a buzz in the air. Not the excited kind you get before a parade or the Harvest Festival, but the sharp-edged kind that made the hairs on the back of my neck stand up.

Murder had a way of turning even the coziest of small towns into something else.

By seven-forty, all the booths were packed, the counter stools were full, and the hum of conversation was louder than the usual clatter of cutlery and clinking coffee mugs. The air was thick with the scent of bacon sizzling on the griddle, brats browning in the pan, and a hint of vanilla from Jacquie's special pancake batter. It smelled like comfort. It tasted like normalcy. But under all that, I could feel the weight of every glance, every whisper.

I took a plate of eggs onto the pass and slid it toward Anthone, who whisked it away with practiced ease. We were in sync, like we always were on busy mornings, but even so, something was off.

Jacquie set down a fresh pot of coffee, nodding toward a booth crammed with retirees talking in low voices. "Everyone's already heard. About Peter Trent. About you."

I sighed. "Figured as much."

Will passed by carrying a menu and a set of silverware, heading toward a booth meant for four but holding five. They were squished together, elbows bumping, but none of them wanted to sit at a separate chair pulled up to the end. People in Nueva Vida tended to stick together when the gossip mill churned at full speed.

"From what I've heard," Will said as he walked past, "the cops might have a long list of suspects. Not just you."

That wasn't exactly reassuring. If I was on the list, it didn't matter who else kept me company.

An hour later, the diner felt like a Sunday crowd, even though we were never open on Sundays. Every inch of space was still full—counter stools, booths, the little two-tops by the windows. The coffee machine worked overtime, and I could feel the heat from the griddle all the way out here. My stomach growled at the aromas, even though I wasn't hungry.

I wiped my hands on my apron and forced my breathing to stay even. "So people know the cops came by?" I asked, keeping my tone light. No need to add fuel to the fire.

Jacquie chuckled as she flipped pancakes onto a plate. "Half the folks in here are watching to see if you break down and confess. The other half are here to show support."

Anthone strode past with a bus tub full of dishes. "And the other half," he said, "are here to tell you all the reasons the cops won't catch the guy."

Jacquie glanced at him, deadpan. "That's three halves."

"People are complicated," Anthone said with a grin. "Doesn't mean I'm wrong."

I smiled faintly, but the knot in my stomach didn't loosen. Maybe it was ridiculous to think the town would treat me any differently. But the old label—murder suspect —wasn't one I wanted hanging over my head again.

"Any useful gossip floating around?" I asked, grabbing a stack of plates. I focused on the work. Plate. Plate. Garnish. Plate. My hands only trembled a little.

"For the cops?" Will asked, coming to stand beside me, his tone easy but his eyes sharp. "Not really. Why? You thinking of sharing?"

I hesitated, then shook my head. Will's past wasn't mine to judge, but I wasn't in the mood to compare notes on our complicated histories with law enforcement. "Only if I learn something that'll help catch the killer," I said. Leaving out the fact that I had every intention of doing my own investigating. "They already know about his complaints about the poutine."

Jacquie slid another plate under the heat lamp and looked at me, eyebrows raised. "You want us to keep our ears open?"

I hesitated again, thinking about Kashvi and Jet. About how I'd barely slept, turning over every possible risk in my head. But Jacquie's question wasn't reckless curiosity. It was loyalty. It was a team effort. They all worked here. They all had something to lose.

And if we didn't figure this out soon, there might not be an EB Eats left to come back to.

"Don't start interrogating anyone," I said, trying to keep my tone light. "But if you hear something useful—facts, not wild guesses—maybe we can pass it along to Kramer and Collett."

Jacquie nodded, but before she could answer, the bell above the door jangled. The room went still for a heartbeat.

Like someone had turned the volume knob down and the air thickened.

Alistair.

He stood in the middle of the diner, chest puffed out like he was about to announce he'd won an award. His gray crew cut was sticking up in uneven tufts, and his chef's jacket was smeared with something that might've been tomato sauce... or maybe something less appetizing.

I sighed.

"Are you sure you should be open?" he called, loud enough that everyone in the diner could hear. A few people turned their heads, more curious than concerned. Most just kept eating.

"Why wouldn't I be?" I asked, wiping my hands on a towel. "It's regular hours. I'm surprised you could get away from your kitchen."

He smirked, clearly pleased he had an audience. "You're about to be arrested for murder," he said, his voice rising with excitement. "The police are going to shut you down."

I took a deep breath. Calm. I was on the high road. Reacting would only make me look defensive—and Alistair wasn't worth it.

"That's news to me," I said evenly. "Where did you get your information?"

He took a step forward, puffed up like an angry rooster. Will and Anthone moved in without me saying a word, flanking me like a couple of bodyguards. Alistair faltered, then stepped back. Smart.

"It's common sense," he blustered. "The man ate here and then died. I can't be the only one making that connection."

"Go back to work, Alistair," Angelica Gordon said from her usual booth by the window. She didn't even look up from her crossword puzzle. "Eliza's not a murderer. That guy didn't die from poison."

Alistair gaped at her, like she'd personally betrayed him. "Fine," he snapped. "You'll all see I was right."

He turned on his heel and shoved the door open hard enough that it banged against the wall. For a second, I worried the old hinges might give out, but they held. Barely.

Angelica waved me over with a flick of her hand. I grabbed the coffee pot and made my way to her booth, pouring without being asked.

"Thanks for backing me up," I said softly.

Angelica gave me a quick smile. "You're good people, Eliza. This town knows a blowhard when it sees one."

"I just don't get why he hates me so much," I said, watching the coffee fill her cup. "I didn't do anything to him."

"You succeeded," she said simply. "Your diner is thriving. His restaurant? Not so much."

That landed heavy. I knew Alistair's place struggled. Maybe that was why he'd decided tearing me down was easier than building himself up.

"We'll keep eating here," Angelica added. "Most of us know better than to believe every rumor we hear."

"Thank you," I said again, quietly. I returned the pot to the counter and set a fresh brew going.

The clatter of plates, the soft murmur of conversation, and the hiss of bacon on the griddle filled the air again, wrapping me up like an old quilt. Maybe things weren't back to normal yet. But they would be.

One cup of coffee, one order of pancakes at a time.

9

The rush at EB Eats slowed by mid-afternoon. Not gone, exactly, but the line at the door had finally disappeared, and my crew had everything running like clockwork again. I handed off the counter to Jacquie, wiped my hands on my apron, and sent a quick text to Kashvi and Jet.

Bringing coffee and treats. Be there in 10.

Kashvi replied with three heart emojis. Jet didn't reply at all, which wasn't unusual. He wasn't a constant texter. But I knew they'd both be there when I arrived.

The air outside was warm for April, but not hot. One of those rare New Mexico days where spring and summer did a little dance together. The breeze smelled faintly of mesquite and honeysuckle. I took a deep breath as I crossed the plaza toward The Open Page. The hand-painted sign above the door swung gently in the breeze.

Of course, they were both there when I walked in. Kashvi was behind the counter, surrounded by a fort of books to be shelved. Jet was lounging in one of the window chairs, scrawling something into a small notebook. As far as

I remembered, he was supposed to be leading a walking tour this afternoon, but when I gave him the raised eyebrow, he just shrugged.

"I'm capable of deciding what to do with my time," he said mildly. "And June Spenser trusts me to show up when it matters."

"Fair enough," I said, setting the coffee tray down on the back table. The donuts came next, a bright pink box from Pan de Vida Bakery. Kashvi let out a small squeal of delight and immediately grabbed one of the chocolate-glazed ones, licking her fingers like she hadn't just put hand sanitizer on three minutes ago.

"I found a couple of things that might help," Kashvi said, her words muffled by donut. "Jet did too."

"All I've got is gossip," I admitted, reaching into the box and choosing an apple fritter for myself. "Some regulars made sure to offer support. And a few shared what they've heard. Not much. No one seems to know where Peter was staying, or why he came here. I guess my regulars don't know everything happening in town."

"They will soon," Jet said, nudging Kashvi's notebook aside to make room for his coffee. "And they'll be begging to tell it to anyone who'll listen. That's good news for us."

I took a sip of my coffee and glanced at the notebooks spread out on the table. Jet's was a mixture of chicken scratch and doodles, Kashvi's all neat handwriting, bullet points, even a few color-coded highlights. Mine was still sitting on my nightstand at home, probably under a cat.

"So," I said. "What did you two find?"

Jet leaned forward, opening his notepad to a dogeared page with the word Suspects in block letters at the top. "I found him on Reddit," he said. "A bunch of posts calling him a liar, scam artist, worse. Whole threads where people warned others not to invest with him."

"Then it turned into people arguing about whether it's his fault or theirs for making dumb investments," Kashvi added, dusting her fingers off over a napkin. "And then the trolls showed up. You know how it goes."

I nodded. It sounded familiar—and depressing.

"Same on a few Facebook groups," Kashvi said. "He's got a pattern. Shows up, convinces people to invest in something, leaves before they figure out they've been scammed."

I let that sink in as I worked on my fritter. Warm cinnamon and apple, fried to just the right crispiness. It didn't make the bad news go down easier, but it didn't hurt either.

"So, motive," I said. "For a lot of people."

"Too many," Jet agreed. "Would be great if we had one clear suspect to point Kramer toward."

"In books, you narrow it down to one or two," I said. "In real life, not so easy. It feels like we're getting nowhere."

Kashvi nudged the donut box toward me again, as if to say have another, but I shook my head. "Anything online about someone threatening him? Revenge posts? Something we could pass to the police?"

"Nothing that felt credible," Kashvi said. "The usual internet rage. But he never replied. Not once."

I frowned. "No defense? Not even a rebuttal?"

"Not a word," Jet said. "He ghosted everyone."

"We should tell Kramer and Collett," I said. "If Peter scammed the wrong person, and they found him here, that's motive and opportunity."

"Wouldn't be hard to track him down if someone was serious," Jet said. "He didn't seem to be hiding very well."

"Maybe one of his old investors moved here," Kashvi said. "Or they're visiting family. Saw him. Snapped."

I let out a breath. "We've found real clues that might point to someone we don't have the capability of finding. Why aren't we calling Kramer right now? Let the police use their resources. Although how about looking for community Facebook groups? The ones where people warn others about scams, traffic problems."

Kashvi smiled like she'd been waiting for me to get there. "You should do it," she said. "And you should call George—not just the police."

I groaned. "Kashvi..."

"Stop," she said, holding up her hands. "I'm serious. You're the one they already talked to. You've got an excuse to be interested."

"She's not wrong," Jet added. "If we call, they'll start wondering why we're poking around. You're already on their radar, but probably not as a real suspect."

"George is eligible," Kashvi said, that grin sneaking back onto her face. "And so are you."

"I'm not flirting with him," I said firmly. "And even if I was—hypothetically—I'm not ready."

Not sure I'd ever be.

Kashvi held her hands up again in mock surrender. "Fine. No flirting. But you should still call."

I looked at Jet. "And if George tells us to back off?"

Jet shrugged. "Then we back off. For now."

I wasn't convinced. "If our guess is right, and Peter scammed someone who decided to take revenge, this just got a whole lot more dangerous. And we have no idea who's who."

"We know," Kashvi said gently. "That's why we're going

to be careful. If George listens, we give him everything we've got. If he doesn't... we regroup."

I sighed. It was the best compromise I was going to get. "I'll call after work," I said. "Maybe I'll have more gossip to pass along by then."

Kashvi raised her coffee cup. "To responsible investigating."

Jet clinked his cup against hers. "And donuts."

I lifted mine last, smiling despite myself. "And not dying."

"Especially that," Kashvi said. "I've got a whole new shipment of books arriving next week. No dying."

We sat there for a little longer, drinking coffee and finishing the donuts, the warmth of the bookstore and the scent of paper and cinnamon settling around us like a safety net. It wasn't much.

But it was enough to keep going.

10

The rest of the day passed in a blur of clinking plates, hissing griddles, and the low hum of gossip floating just below the surface of every conversation. Some of it was whispered, some of it not so much. Shift change had come and gone by the time I made it back from my meeting with Jet and Kashvi, and the afternoon crew was in full swing.

Lissa and Lola picked up where Will and Anthone had left off—handing me tidbits of rumor in between running plates and refilling coffee mugs. Most of what they'd heard was the same stuff as the morning: speculation, worry, and the usual "I heard from my cousin who heard from the lady at the bakery who swears it's true" sort of thing.

I relieved Jacquie in the kitchen and lost myself in the rhythm of cooking. Burgers sizzled on the flat top. Fries crisped in the basket. The familiar sounds and smells of the diner settled over me like a well-worn quilt. Out there in the dining room, people smiled and laughed. In here, I stayed busy and quiet.

For a little while, it was almost like things were normal.

An hour before closing, during the quiet lull between dinner and what I always called "snack o'clock," I stepped out onto the back porch, phone in hand, and dialed Detective Kramer.

He picked up on the second ring. "Kramer."

"I have some information for you," I said without preamble. Better to get it out fast before he told me to mind my own business.

There was a pause. "Eliza," he said, voice steady. "Let us handle the investigating."

He didn't sound annoyed. If anything, there was concern layered into those words, and it threw me off balance for a second. I could handle anger. Concern was something else entirely. It made me think of someone looking out for me, and I didn't know how to feel about that.

"I'm not trying to do your job," I said, keeping my tone as polite as I could manage. "Most of this is just things I've heard from my customers. The sort of people who won't exactly call you up and share what they know."

He was silent again, probably weighing whether I was a pain or an asset. I decided to push, gently.

"You'd be surprised what you hear when people think you're not listening," I added. "And gossip can lead to real information."

Finally, he exhaled. "You have a point," he admitted. "Why don't you come down to the station after you close up?"

I glanced at the back door to the diner. Through the little window, I could see Lola wiping down a table while Lissa restocked the napkin dispensers. I didn't want to leave them to finish on their own. And I didn't want to be seen walking into the station, either.

"Better idea," I said. "Why don't you and your partner come by the diner? After closing. No audience."

There was a muffled conversation on his end. I couldn't make out the words, but I caught a woman's voice—Collett, probably. Then Kramer came back on the line.

"We could use a good meal," he said. "Eight o'clock?"

"Eight works." I tried not to overthink the little flutter in my stomach.

That was nerves.

Definitely nerves.

"And we can't accept a freebie," he added. "If that was part of the offer."

I smiled. "I'll keep the register open. No freebies." I hadn't planned on giving away food. Well, maybe a little extra on their plates, but that was just good hospitality. Still, I appreciated the reminder. Clean lines. No favors.

I hung up and stared at the phone in my hand. One hour forty-five minutes. That's how long I had to figure out how to present what we'd found without making it obvious we'd been poking around on our own. We were "pausing" our investigation, after all. I didn't want him to tell me—officially or otherwise—to back off.

The last hour passed in a haze of wiping counters, refilling ketchup bottles, and nodding at regulars who'd stayed late over pie and coffee. Lissa and Lola kept things moving, their energy easing the weight in my chest.

As a business owner, I appreciated the full tables. As someone who didn't want murder to be the reason for my success, I was less thrilled.

"Last one's out," Lola called from the front door. She gave me a wink. "I locked it. No stragglers."

"Thanks," I said, setting the coffee pot back on its warmer.

"One more thing," she added, turning to lean against the counter. "There's a guy at the motel who says he knew Peter. Said he was a crook."

I set the mug I was drying down slowly. "Name? Description?"

"Nope." Lola shrugged. "Just said 'a guy.' I figured the detectives could sort that out. Honestly, if I wrote crime fiction, I'd be thrilled right now. This stuff is gold. Well, I mean—" She winced. "You know. If someone hadn't died and all."

"I get it," I said, smiling faintly. "Let's hope the detectives find that guy before anyone else does."

She grinned. "I've got an invitation to a writing retreat next month. Maybe this'll be my next book."

I didn't comment. Instead, I told them both I could handle cleanup on my own. "I've got guests coming," I added. I hadn't promised Kramer secrecy, but it seemed better not to advertise who was showing up for dinner.

We split tips, as we always did at the end of the day— though I just handled the receipts, no tip for the owner. Lissa and Lola counted out cash and tallied the credit card tips while I cleaned off the counter. Three envelopes went into the register for Jacquie, Anthone, and Will. We didn't split tips by shift—never had. Everyone worked for the team.

"I can help clean," Lissa offered, wiping her hands on a towel.

"I'm good," I said, meaning it. "Go home. Enjoy your evening."

Lola was already halfway out the door, waving over her shoulder. Lissa hesitated for another second, then handed me her apron and left too.

By eight, I'd wiped down every table twice and polished

the counter for good measure. I'd set two places at the far end of the counter where they could eat without feeling on display. The coffee was fresh, and the last batch of corn-bread was keeping warm in the oven.

The clock ticked past eight-twenty, and for a minute, I wondered if they'd gotten tied up with something more important. Maybe they were out arresting the killer right now.

Maybe they'd changed their minds.

I was just about to turn off the lights when the bell over the door jingled. Detective Kramer and Detective Collett stepped inside.

11

They didn't look much different from earlier. Kramer still had that tired, slightly rumpled appearance that made me wonder if he slept in his car. His tie was askew, his jacket open. Collett looked sharp enough to cut glass, and I could feel her eyes tracking everything as she walked in.

I reminded myself I'd invited them.

"Hope you're hungry," I said, keeping my tone easy. "I've got chili and cornbread, or you can have a burger if you prefer."

Kramer gave me a faint smile. "Chili sounds good."

Collett nodded, saying nothing, and took the stool beside him at the counter.

I poured them both coffee without asking and set the cups down with practiced ease. They both doctored their cups before I slid bowls of chili under the heat lamp and dropped two slabs of cornbread on small plates. I left the kitchen to add honey butter to each and carried the servings over.

Kramer waited until I'd set everything down before he spoke again. "You said you had information."

I glanced at Collett. Her expression hadn't changed. She might have been carved from stone.

"I do," I said. "Some of it's probably not news to you. Some might be."

Collett set her spoon down. "We don't encourage civilian investigations, Ms. Burton."

I held up a hand. "I'm not investigating. I'm listening. People tell me things they wouldn't tell you."

Kramer nodded slowly. "We're listening now."

I kept it simple. Told them what I'd learned about Peter Trent—his history of scamming people, the social media posts Jet and Kashvi had found, the angry threads on Reddit. I mentioned the man at the motel who supposedly knew Trent and called him a crook. I left out the fact that Kashvi and Jet were involved. No need to complicate things.

Kramer ate while I talked. Collett didn't touch her food while I spoke, making notes instead.

"He was here to scam someone," I finished. "Or maybe to hide. Either way, he made enemies."

Kramer wiped his mouth with a napkin. "We already knew about his reputation."

"I figured," I said. "But if people here knew who he was, that makes motive easier to find."

"Do you have any names?" Collett asked.

"No." I met her gaze. "But I'll let you know if I hear any."

She frowned, but Kramer nodded again, slower this time. "We'll talk to the manager at the motel. Thanks for the heads-up."

I poured more coffee without being asked. "People are scared," I said. "And worried. They want this solved fast."

"We're doing our best," Collett said, digging her spoon

into the bowl. "Which would be easier if people weren't speculating."

I didn't argue. No point.

Kramer finished his chili and leaned back slightly. "You've lived through this before."

It wasn't a question. And I wasn't sure how I felt about him bringing it up.

"I have," I said. "Which is why I don't want to do it again."

He studied me. "Then stay out of it."

I gave him a half-smile. "We both know that's not going to happen."

Collett stood, pushing her half-eaten chili away. "We'll be in touch."

Kramer stood too, leaving cash on the counter. More than enough to cover the meal.

"Thanks for the chili," he said.

"Anytime," I said, and I meant it. I wasn't ready to trust them, but I didn't think they were the enemy.

They left without another word. I locked the door behind them and leaned against it for a second, letting out a slow breath.

I hadn't told them everything. But I'd told them enough for now. The question was whether it would help—or get me in deeper.

12

The next morning, I was elbow-deep in pancake batter when Kashvi texted.

Jet says meet at the bookstore after lunch. Got something.

I didn't have time to reply. The Saturday brunch crowd was packed into EB Eats like it was the last diner on Earth. Every stool at the counter was full. Every booth had a wait-list. The kitchen hummed with the kind of controlled chaos that made me both tired and proud.

Anthone handled the griddle like a pro, flipping pancakes and eggs without breaking a sweat. Jacquie moved between stations with the precision of someone who knew exactly how long every plate would take to come together.

I stayed on coffee duty and helped Lola keep the front running smoothly. Will handled the register, charming customers with that lopsided smile of his. Even Lissa had stayed late to help. It was the kind of teamwork that made me feel like we might survive this—if we could just get past the part where people thought I might be a murderer.

By two, the crowd thinned enough for me to breathe. I

left Jacquie, Anthone, and Will to handle the diners and headed toward The Open Page.

The bell above the door chimed softly as I stepped inside. Kashvi was behind the counter, sorting a stack of new releases, and Jet sat cross-legged on the floor with his laptop open in front of him.

"We found his reservation," Kashvi said as soon as I was close enough.

I blinked. "What?"

"Trent," Jet said. "From the motel. The owner said he checked in under a fake name, but they got his real one when he paid in cash and left a business card for 'Future Investments.'"

Kashvi rolled her eyes. "Subtle."

I sank into the chair next to Jet. "So now what?"

"Now," Kashvi said, "we figure out who he met with. The owner says he had a couple of visitors. One matched Alistair's description."

I frowned. "Alistair?"

Jet nodded. "No confirmation, but it sounds like him."

I shook my head. "That doesn't make sense. Alistair's a jerk, but murder?"

"Desperation makes people do stupid things," Kashvi said quietly.

I didn't like where this was going. If Alistair was involved, it complicated everything.

"We need proof," I said.

Jet grinned. "Already working on it. The owner has security footage. He's willing to let us look—if we ask nicely."

I sighed. "I'll go. If we decide it's a good idea. I just feel a bit like we're treading on George's toes. And now they know where he stayed, they'll be on top of it."

Kashvi and Jet exchanged a glance, but neither argued.

We ended up agreeing to keep looking online and leave the security footage to the authorities. I headed back to the diner.

13

D oing research between feeding my diners and chatting with my staff wasn't exactly productive. Every time I stopped scrolling to fill an order, I lost the thread. But it was the only time I had, so I made do.

Jacquie had headed out for a rare afternoon commitment, leaving me glued to the flat top. I loved cooking, but after a few hours, the heat turned oppressive, and the air smelled like grilled food layered with a faint hint of dishwasher chemicals. Not exactly inspiring.

I propped my phone by the sink. In the quick gaps between orders, I grabbed sips of water and squeezed in a search or two. I could only hope Jet and Kashvi were getting further than I was.

Will passed me an order slip for poutine. "I talked to the family."

I hadn't planned to bring it up. He wasn't a kid—not technically—and even if he was in my eyes, he wasn't *my* kid.

"How'd they take it?"

He shrugged, grabbing a basket for the fries. "Told

them I wasn't going to do it. I can't risk getting dragged back in. No one would trust me. They didn't give me an order, though—never do. Just the old 'think about your path in life' speech. Pretty much the same way the elders talk."

Relief washed over me, as sudden and shocking as stepping into the walk-in cooler.

"The cops asked me again last night. If you care about my opinion, I think you made the right call."

I slid the bowls of cheesy, gravy-drenched fries onto the pass-through. Will sprinkled cilantro on top and added the obligatory condiment selection in Nueva Vida—four kinds of hot sauce.

"The gang needs to be taken down," he said quietly. "I can't do it. But someone needs to. Maybe I can talk to the cops, help them figure out a plan."

It sounded like he had a plan already. But before I could press him, he was off, delivering the order.

I peered through the service hatch. Only one table was occupied. Normally, I'd sneak out back to cool off in the alley. Not today. Instead, I wet a cloth at the sink and wiped my face, hoping to clear my head. No luck. Will's future still tugged at the edges of my mind.

I shifted to the side of the pass-through where no one could see me and picked up my phone. Social media was Jet and Kashvi's territory. I didn't trust myself not to fall down a rabbit hole of baby goat videos, so I hit the regular search engines.

I started by searching Peter Trent with the same conditions that found him before. It didn't take long to find his LinkedIn profile—his picture was a photo I could work with. A reverse image search pulled up more hits. Sometimes I wonder how we did anything before smartphones.

Then again, maybe we just didn't. I wouldn't be investigating a murder if it weren't for the internet.

"The tables are clear," Lola said, popping her head into the kitchen. "I'll take my break now, if that's okay? Back in thirty."

If things went as usual, we'd have an hour or so of lull time before the dinner rush. A couple of regulars would wander in for coffee and free Wi-Fi, but it would be slow.

"No problem. Want me to put up a burger for you?" Staff meals were free during shift. And, honestly, even when they weren't.

"I'm going for a walk," she said. "Scouting locations for my next book."

"Good luck." I set my phone down. With Will out front alone, it didn't feel right digging through internet results. The dishwasher needed emptying. Counters needed wiping. And the condiment tubs looked low. I grabbed cilantro, tomatoes, and lemons from the cooler.

Will was checking on our one occupied table when the door chime jingled. Cassidey walked in. She made a beeline for Will and said something too low for me to catch.

Will glanced my way, silent question in his eyes.

"Grilled cheese coming up," I called. "How about I make two?"

He steered Cassidey to a booth against the wall, then came over to the window.

"I can't take my break, but I don't need lunch. Put hers on my tab."

"No need," I said. "Lola'll be back in ten, and I can handle the non-existent rush. Your friend can have lunch on me once in a while."

I gave him a mock glare, and he grinned before filling two glasses at the soda fountain.

I wondered if he was still trying to help her get out of the gang. I trusted him. Mostly. But every connection he had to that world made me worry for him.

"Lola's on her way," Will said as he picked up the sandwiches. "I won't be long. Cassidey and I have stuff to work out."

That did nothing to ease my mind.

I finished the prep, reloaded the condiments, and emptied the dishwasher. Then I picked up my phone again, still keeping half an eye on the dining area. The diners. The door. And Will and Cassidey. All more important than chasing down Peter Trent, con man.

Two minutes later, Lola returned, a bag full of dead branches and stones slung over her shoulder.

"You can see better from the other side of the passthrough," she said. "Let me drop these out back and I'll take over."

In the alley, we had a tiny café table and a couple of chairs for breaks without diners watching. It was our refuge.

"Will you ever feel comfortable letting those two sit out there alone?" Lola asked as she washed her hands and tied her apron. "Give them a little privacy. Young love is fragile."

Love? That hadn't crossed my mind. I thought they were connected by circumstance, not romance.

"Not up to me," I said. "He hasn't asked. I'm not going to offer."

Before I could step out front, Lola caught my arm. "One more thing. Something I heard."

Lola wasn't a gossip. If she was bringing something up, it mattered. For a second, I braced myself—was Alistair running his mouth again?

"I heard from Katie," she said. "You know her? Runs the cleaning service?"

"Yeah. Comes in for lunch sometimes." Always sitting at the counter, chatting up anyone and everyone.

"She was talking to Mrs. Waverly. I overheard because Katie was practically yelling."

Mrs. Waverly didn't miss much with those hearing aids of hers, but I guess some people see old and think deaf.

"Alistair's been spreading rumors," Lola said. "About your ex. That he died under suspicious circumstances. I told her not to believe him."

I wanted to say it wasn't true. But lying to Lola wouldn't work. The story wouldn't die, and Alistair had just enough facts to make it stick.

"He was murdered," I said quietly. "By a criminal."

I saw the spark of curiosity in her eyes. Telling a writer your secrets was always risky. They had a tendency to turn you into a character, even if you barely recognized yourself.

"My ex-husband was a criminal," I added. "He knew Peter Trent. I didn't kill either of them."

Lola grinned. "Never thought you did. But all this drama has me itching to write romantic suspense."

I laughed, mostly with relief. When she headed for the kitchen, I pocketed my phone and went to check on the table of diners. I'd have time for more digging before close.

14

The door chime rang at seven-thirty. One more hungry diner. So much for a quick close and a run to the bookstore to meet Kashvi and Jet for an evening of investigating.

I glanced up from the griddle I was scouring and found Detective George Kramer sliding onto a stool at the counter, directly across from the pass-through.

Perfect. I'd bet money on him being here for more than just a bite to eat.

Will handed him a menu anyway. "We're closing in half an hour," he said, laying out a roll of napkin and cutlery.

"I know when you're open," George replied. He took off his coat and hat, draping them over the next stool like he planned to stay awhile.

"I need a word with you and Ms. Burton. Thought I'd do it over a meal. What do you recommend?"

I didn't wait for Will to answer. As the cook, I was well aware of what wouldn't leave me with a mountain of extra dishes.

"You probably remember from the other day—the chili's good. I can do a burger or anything on the griddle."

"I'll take the chili. And a Coke," George said.

I ladled up a generous bowl and topped it with cheese, chilies, and onions. No cornbread left, but I threw some tortillas into the fryer and called it close enough. Will set the drink beside him with a paper straw.

"I'll help Lola clean," Will said. Then, turning to George, he added, "You and I can talk after we finish closing. Eliza's ready now."

That flicker of worry I always carried for Will dimmed a little. If he could talk to a cop like that—steady and sure— maybe he wouldn't be so easily dragged into something dangerous.

"Where are you with the investigation?" I asked, turning off the griddle and scraping it before it cooled too much.

George took a spoonful of chili before answering. "Can't talk about an ongoing investigation."

Right. The usual line. He took another bite, nodding like the chili was a revelation.

"You should stick to making food like this," he added. "And stay out of my work. It's dangerous, chasing down a killer."

I sprayed cleaner across the griddle, scrubbing harder than necessary.

"Sounds to me like you haven't made much progress. That whole 'I can't talk' spiel is just a cover."

He crushed a handful of tortilla chips into the bowl and stirred. I tried not to wince. Soggy chips. Some crimes were unforgivable.

"You know," George said, still focused on his bowl, "Killers often try to get involved in investigations."

I didn't answer. Not because I didn't have something to

say, but because if I opened my mouth, I might start yelling. I checked the fryer oil instead, deciding to change it in the morning. It was still hot from frying those poor, ruined tortilla chips. In the morning, it'd be cold and safer to pour into the vat for recycling or whatever they do with it.

He waited me out. I let him. The dishwasher hummed as I loaded in the last of the prep pans. We still had about fifteen minutes of work to get through after he left, but at least the dirtiest part was done.

"You think I'm a killer?" I asked, wiping my hands on a towel. He hadn't said it outright, but his comment landed like an accusation.

He scraped the bottom of the bowl clean, then drained his Coke. I guess we were both playing the delay game now. I was better at it.

"No," he said at last. "But like I said, whoever did this is dangerous. We do have some leads. Denise is following up on his hotel... or whatever. We have security videos. Got anything from your nosy poking around? Before you step back."

There it was again. That mix of rudeness and restraint. I still wasn't sure why I bothered talking to him. Maybe because he was the only cop who talked back.

"Other than that he was staying at the motel? No," I said. Short answers felt safer. And it wasn't a lie. Not really.

He grunted. It could've meant anything—okay, I don't believe you, or we'll see. "A murder case can't be rushed. I'll do what I can to clear your name with the gossips."

That made me snort.

"Unless you're planning to stand outside with a bullhorn and announce I'm innocent, it won't make much difference."

His mouth twitched like he wanted to smile, but he didn't. Just stood and adjusted his coat.

Will went through the kitchen door, balancing a tub of dishes. "That's the last of it."

I glanced out front. Empty. "I'll get the door. Five minutes early won't make a difference."

I hoped George would take the hint. But instead of heading out when I locked the door, he turned to Will.

"Okay, kid," George said. "I get that you don't want to talk to me. But there's no point in my waiting around. You know what we want from you?" There was something reluctant in his voice now, something that made me think this wasn't his idea. That cooled some of my irritation.

Will glanced at me. I didn't give him anything. We'd already talked it through. I needed him to trust his own decisions. And I needed to trust him to be the adult he technically was. Someday, maybe, I would.

"I won't go back to the gang," Will said. His voice was steady. Calm. His whole body language was... controlled. Someone had coached him on this. Maybe Lola. Maybe Cassidey, but I doubted that. Maybe it came from his own hard-won experience.

George nodded slowly. "What about pointing us in the direction of someone who might help?"

"No one I know will risk it," Will said. He turned to leave.

"Not even that Cassidey girl?"

Will's face darkened. His jaw clenched tight. I could almost hear the internal war he was fighting to keep his hands open and his voice level.

He won.

He looked down at his hands, slowly uncurling them from fists. Then he raised his eyes to George. "Getting out of that gang was the hardest thing I've ever done. They put me in the hospital for a week for leaving. Cassidey's trying to escape too. If you put her in danger, I'll throw everything away to keep her safe. If you need help with the gang, put a cop undercover."

I cheered him in my head. Calm. Focused. Strong.

George sighed. "That gang is hurting people. Threatening kids. Maybe they aren't selling drugs yet, but they will. I've seen it before. It's always the same."

"I never did any of that," Will said quietly. "What they do now, or in the future, isn't my problem. Or Cassidey's." He turned away and walked to the booth where Lola waited. She whispered something, and her hand settled on his shoulder. Steadying him.

I turned to George. "I think it's time you left."

For a second, I thought he'd argue. But he just picked up his hat and coat and headed for the door. He tossed a twenty on the counter as he passed.

Then he stopped. "You're right," he said. "I'm not going to convince you it's too dangerous. Just stay out of our way."

And then he left.

15

I wasn't in the mood to bundle into the back room of Kashvi's bookstore tonight, so I texted them to come over to my place instead. We'd have more room to talk. More wine, too. Plus, I had enchiladas I made yesterday —comfort food ready to reheat.

And best of all, I could wear something cozy that didn't smell like grilled onions and fryer oil. Bonus points for quality time with Macchiato.

She met me at the door the second I got home, winding around my ankles with a little chirrup that told me she was unimpressed by how long I'd been gone. I scooped her up and rubbed behind her ears until she gave me the grudging purr that meant I was forgiven—for now.

In the fifteen minutes between my text and their knock at the door, I set the oven to warm the enchiladas, showered, changed into sweats, and worked on letting go of the anger George Kramer had stirred up. His disregard for Will's safety grated. His regard for mine grated even more.

Macchiato padded silently into the kitchen as I slid the

tray into the oven, then jumped up onto her spot on the windowsill. She watched me like I might forget to feed her, even though her bowl was half full. A low tail flick told me she wasn't thrilled with enchilada night. She preferred tuna.

Will had promised both me and Lola that he was fine. He apologized for getting angry and finished closing without a fuss. The kid was still raw. I wasn't about to scold him for the emotions he couldn't keep locked down. And I wasn't about to tell him I'd have decked George, either. It was too soon to offer comfort. Too soon to offer Cassidey a safe place, even if I knew of one—which I didn't. As long as she stayed tied to the Devil Dogs, my hands were tied too.

The enchiladas were cooling on the counter when Kashvi and Jet arrived. The warm aroma of tomatoes, spices, and corn made my kitchen feel a little less heavy. Macchiato hopped down from her perch and sat in the doorway, watching them with bright, curious eyes.

"She's giving us the royal inspection," Jet said as he stepped inside.

"She's not sure about you," I said. "But she likes you enough not to run and hide."

Kashvi crouched and held out a hand. "Hello, gorgeous."

Macchiato sniffed her fingers, then butted her head against Kashvi's knuckles, graciously accepting the welcome. She wasn't much for strangers, but Kashvi passed muster. Jet earned a brief stare and a slow blink—approval, in Macchiato terms.

I poured wine while Jet served the food. Another reason to meet here: real plates, real forks, and a table that wasn't sticky no matter how many times I wiped it.

Macchiato leapt lightly onto her chair at the table—the one she considered hers—and curled up like she was about to contribute something brilliant to our investigation.

"Did you find anything?" Jet asked as he set a plate in front of me.

I grabbed my phone, guilt bubbling up. With the lunch rush, Will's situation, and Kramer's oh-so-helpful visit, I'd completely forgotten to follow up on the reverse image search.

"Give me a sec." A few taps later, there it was. "Looks like there was a court case."

I sent them both the link. "Johns Ferry, northern California. Fraud charges."

"Not a surprise," Kashvi said, tapping at her own phone. "Nice to have confirmation Peter Trent was a con man. Let's see if there's more."

"I've got it," Jet said, his thumbs flying. "Charges were dropped."

He didn't bother sending a link—he just read aloud. "From a more recent article, week after the first. Gotta love small-town papers. They actually follow up."

"Only because they don't have a lot of scandals," Kashvi muttered. "Where'd you find it?"

"Same paper." Jet shrugged. "The charges were dropped for lack of proof. The complainants withdrew their accusations."

"Too bad we don't have their names," I said. "Maybe he settled with them to shut it down."

Macchiato gave a tiny huff, like she didn't approve of people taking the easy way out. She stretched, then settled again, her tail wrapping around her paws.

"At least we have confirmation he was dirty," Kashvi said.

"Any other connections?" I asked, hopeful.

Jet shook his head. "A couple, but no names. Kind of amazing he got anyone to buy in, honestly. A quick search should've thrown red flags. You'd think people would be more skeptical these days."

"They are," Kashvi said. "At least here in Nueva Vida. After the old sheriff."

I blinked. "What about the old sheriff?"

I hadn't done much digging when I moved here. I made sure the diner wasn't a money pit and that I had enough clientele to stay afloat. I hadn't looked into old scandals. Maybe I should have.

"Yeah," Kashvi said slowly. "We don't talk about it much. It's in the past, and the new sheriff's cleaning up the mess. That's why George is here. The old lead detective got appointed sheriff, and they brought George in from Santa Fe."

"And started a training program," Jet added. "New blood. Fresh starts."

I didn't mind going off track. Sometimes the side roads were where you found what mattered. "So what happened?"

Jet topped up our wine and pushed his phone aside. This was going to be more than a soundbite.

Macchiato, who had been quietly observing, hopped down from her chair and rubbed her cheek against my leg before settling at my feet. Warm and solid. A little anchor.

"We had our own real-life version of one of those corrupt southern cop stories," Jet said. "Wasn't as bad as the movies make it out. But it wasn't a comedy, either."

Kashvi picked up the thread. "The sheriff was skimming from the budget, taking bribes, locking people up because he didn't like them. It all came out when he got sloppy. His victims are still dealing with the trauma."

It explained the way George and Denise operated. By the book, no shortcuts. And it explained George's determination to shut the gang down.

"So that's why he's pushing so hard on the Devil Dogs," I said.

Jet chuckled, which earned him a look from Kashvi and an eyebrow from me. "I'm not laughing at the gang," he said. "Just... anywhere else they'd be called a bunch of hooligans. They wouldn't be a police priority."

"They damaged Will," Kashvi snapped. "They nearly killed him when he tried to leave."

"I know," Jet said gently. Then he turned to me, his voice dropping as if someone might be listening through the windows. "When Will tried to leave the first time, he came to me. I took him camping. It took a few days, but he finally told me everything."

I nodded, letting him talk. Macchiato gave a soft trill, as if to say listen up, and I scratched behind her ears.

"He didn't want to go to the elders. He was ashamed. But I got the picture. The Devil Dogs are classic bullies. They take money for 'protection,' mostly from kids and small businesses. They've picked up some real gang behavior— tattoos, beatings, intimidation."

"They're a gateway," Kashvi said. "And George doesn't want them to get worse."

"Exactly," Jet said. "If the cops keep busting them for misdemeanors without offering a way out, it leaves a vacuum for real criminals to move in." He opened another bottle of wine. We were going to need it.

I let out a breath. "So our side project, after we solve this murder, is what? Shut them down?"

"Shut down the Devil Dogs?" Kashvi asked.

I shook my head in disbelief. "Sounds like a bad West Side Story revival."

Macchiato flicked her tail like she agreed.

"No," I said. "Help the cops shut them down without turning them into actual criminals."

Jet lifted his glass. "To side projects."

Kashvi clinked hers against ours. "And to doing it right."

Macchiato didn't toast, but she did stretch out a paw and pat my foot once. A small reminder that home, for now, was safe.

16

"We found three names," Kashvi said, pulling us back on track. "Your idea to check the community Facebook groups was brilliant. We found four just for Nueva Vida. Three people posted almost identical warnings about a con man."

"This has to be something Denise Collett would've found," I said, half to myself. Surely the police were better at social media sleuthing than civilians. Or was I giving them too much credit?

"Maybe," Kashvi said as she scrolled through her phone. "But if they haven't figured out he was a con man—sorry, was a con man—then maybe they aren't looking for him the same way we are."

I thought back, past my annoyance with George Kramer's warning to stay out of it, to what little he'd shared.

"I didn't get much from George. He said Denise was looking for where Peter stayed. I told him about the motel. But if no one's sharing what they know with the detectives, how can they be expected to solve the murder?"

"They need to earn the community's respect," Jet said

from the kitchen, where he stacked our empty wine glasses in the sink. "We're going to get more from gossip than George or Denise will by asking directly. I'm guessing Trent didn't check in under his real name—or list 'grifter' as his occupation. Now they know he was at the motel, we can let them handle the follow-up."

He wasn't wrong, and we'd agreed to do just that.

"So we focus on the names we found," I said. "Do I know any of them?"

Kashvi glanced up from her phone.

"Woody Howell, Tina Ingles, and Norma Jackson."

"They all go to the same church," Jet added as he returned to the table. "But I'm not sure they're close friends."

"What caught our attention was the wording," Kashvi said. "No names, but if you know what to look for..."

Jet slid his phone across the table toward me. "See for yourself."

I picked it up. Three posts, word for word: *New guy in town. Got a lot of ideas. Don't believe what you can't prove.*

I frowned. "You think they got together and agreed on this?"

"Sure looks like it," Jet said, reclaiming his phone. "They're probably warning people offline, too."

"Are they suspects?" I asked, knowing it was too easy to be true. But still.

"I can't picture any of them stabbing someone," Jet replied.

Macchiato stretched out along the windowsill behind Kashvi, her paws tucked under her chest like she was listening. She yawned, flicked her tail once, and gave me a look that said, Ask the right questions, human.

I took a breath. "Why wouldn't they go to the cops

instead of hinting online?" Even as I asked, I already knew the answer.

"The old sheriff," Kashvi said. "All three of them had run-ins with Jackson back in the day. They're old enough to hold grudges, and no, I don't have details."

Macchiato hopped off the sill and padded over to my lap, headbutting my hand until I scratched behind her ears. Her purr rumbled against my wrist—steady, grounding.

"We need to talk to them," Kashvi went on. "Set up interviews."

I glanced at the clock. It was closing in on ten. In an hour, I'd be falling asleep at the table. "Too late to call them now."

"Maybe we should pass this on to George," Jet said. "And by 'we,' I mean you, Eliza. Pretty sure he doesn't know we're helping you out."

"Yet," Kashvi added with a grin. "Jet and I are like undercover private investigators."

"Why do I feel like the scapegoat?" Or maybe the decoy while Kashvi tried to set me up with George. I wasn't sure which idea was worse.

"Think of it like you're the front woman for a rock band," Kashvi said. "You're the star."

I snorted. "I don't feel like a star. More like the person everyone blames when the amp blows."

Macchiato gave a soft mrrp, as if to agree, then leapt lightly onto her chair at the table. She sat like a queen watching over her court, tail curled neatly around her feet.

"I don't want to hand over the names yet," I said after a pause. "We should talk to these people first. Make sure it's worth the risk of getting their names on some kind of official list." And giving them a reason to hate me.

Jet nodded. "We don't know for sure they were talking about Peter Trent."

"Or if they were warning people about someone else," I finished the thought. "I don't want to alienate anyone in town. I'm trying to build something here, not burn bridges."

Kashvi gave a solemn nod. "Tomorrow's Sunday. You're off all day. Most of my customers are in church until noon," she said. "I don't open until the afternoon."

Jet stood and grabbed both their jackets. "I've got a walking tour that wraps up around one. If you set up the meetings for two or later, I'll be there."

We finished the night with Kashvi agreeing to call all three people and arrange something. I promised to meet her at the bookstore in the morning to help, even though there weren't that many calls to make. I just didn't want to sit around doing nothing until afternoon. Sure, I had paperwork for the diner, but solving a murder felt slightly more pressing.

Macchiato hopped back onto her perch on the windowsill as I walked Jet and Kashvi out. She stayed there, silhouetted by the porch light, keeping watch as they headed down the driveway.

"See you tomorrow," Jet called.

"Bright and early," Kashvi added with a grin.

I waved them off and closed the door behind me.

Cleanup was quick. I loaded the dishwasher, wiped down the counters, and checked Macchiato's water bowl before settling at the table again. She jumped up beside me, pressing her side against my leg as I opened my laptop for a quick search on our three potential leads.

Nothing too deep. Just enough to put faces to names.

Macchiato stretched out across my lap as I typed, her tail

flicking lazily. Warm and steady. Just what I needed before turning in.

17

I brought muffins and coffee with me when I joined Kashvi at the bookstore. Same ones we sold at the diner—there were a few things we didn't make ourselves because baking was an entirely different job from cooking. Besides, our baker had a talent I couldn't fake, and I was fine with that.

Hauling in the oversized coffee traveler and the box of muffins reminded me I needed to follow up on the food festival planned for fall. Nueva Vida wasn't exactly a foodie mecca, but between the restaurants and cafés, we covered a good range of cuisines.

And with the town's bylaw banning food trucks, the annual festival was the one time of year everyone could set up in the park with grills and coolers and hand out teaser bites. It was as close as we got to a food scene, and I had a feeling it'd be the perfect time for Anthone to test out his new skills and see how much work was involved in being the boss.

Kashvi locked the front door behind me.

"Back room," she said, nodding toward the rear. "I haven't made any calls yet."

"Won't they all be at church?" I asked, setting the coffee down on the desk with a thump. Most of Nueva Vida seemed to spend Sunday mornings in a pew somewhere. It was why I didn't open the diner on Sundays anymore. I could cook all I wanted, but trying to get people to change their after-church lunch habits was an uphill battle I wasn't interested in fighting.

"They should all be home by eleven-thirty," Kashvi said as she grabbed mugs from a shelf. "We've got time to plan what we're asking. Can't just call them cold. And we can't sound like telemarketers."

"And we shouldn't drink all this coffee before we do anything," I said as I set out the muffins. "Jitters make people nervous."

She grinned and poured us each a full cup anyway. "You bought enough coffee for an entire board meeting."

"Figured we'd need the fuel," I said, peeling back the wrapper of a muffin. "You never know what we're walking into. And you have a microwave for when it gets cold."

Kashvi took a blueberry muffin and broke off a piece. "How much do you know about our subjects?"

"All of them come into the diner now and then," I said. "That's about it. Am I a bad neighbor?"

She shrugged. "Not bad. Just... new. Nueva Vida is a small town. You can't rely on great food to keep people loyal. You need to show up. Take sides."

I frowned. "Sides?"

"Not like that," she said, laughing. "It's not violent. Well —except that time Mrs. Waverly decided the Baptists had a bigger stall than the Catholics at the harvest fair."

I raised a brow. "What happened?"

"She threw a cupcake at their sign," Kashvi said, trying not to laugh. "The Baptists retaliated with a banana cream pie. Straight into the Catholic bunting."

I tried not to picture it. Failed. And laughed until I couldn't breathe.

"Well, at least they stuck to desserts," I finally gasped out.

"Exactly." Kashvi took another bite of her muffin. "But it's that kind of thing. People want to know where you stand. Even if it's something ridiculous like what color flowers you put in your window boxes."

"So, I have to pick a team?" I asked. "Because it sounds like whatever I do, I'll alienate half my customers."

"You won't lose them," Kashvi said. "But you'll stay an outsider until you pick something to stand for. Anything. It's not about agreeing with them, it's about showing you care."

I let that settle for a moment. She was right. My life had been all about buying the diner, keeping it running, and staying afloat. It was time to put down roots that weren't just tied to the cash register.

"So," I said, "any feuds between our three interview subjects?"

"Not right now," Kashvi said. "Woody Howell is a retired accountant. Plays gin rummy and cribbage. Norma Jackson used to be a nurse. She's pretty judgy—probably best not to mention the other two around her unless you want her to react."

"Like if she doesn't want to meet, we tell her Woody's already agreed, so she doesn't want to be left out?" I said. "Feels like we're arranging playdates."

"Welcome to small-town diplomacy," Kashvi said, scrolling through her contacts. "And yeah, that's exactly how it works."

"You've got everyone in your phone?" I asked. "Is the town really that small?"

She grinned. "They're all customers. I make it my business to know the people who buy or borrow my books."

I took another sip of coffee. "What about Tina?"

"She keeps to herself," Kashvi said. "She was a guidance counselor at the high school. Probably gave all the advice she's got in her. Doesn't mean she won't have an opinion, though."

We decided to call Woody first. Kashvi figured he was bored enough to say yes, and since she knew him better, she'd make the call while I stayed quiet. Using speaker was common enough that no one would question it, and it let me listen in without raising suspicion.

"Woody Howell," came the voice, crackling just a little through the line.

"Hey, Woody. It's Kashvi Patel."

"Morning," he said. "What's on your mind?"

"I'm calling about Peter Trent," she said. "You posted something about a new guy in town? Thought maybe you'd be willing to talk to us."

"You chasing the police?" Woody asked bluntly. "I told them what I know. If you're acting for them, some kind of check on my honesty, you can stop wasting your time."

I sat up a little straighter. That was news. George and Denise had clearly been working the case more than they were letting on.

"We're looking into it separately," Kashvi said smoothly. "Not gonna lie—we're not sure the new detectives know enough about the people they're supposed to protect to figure this one out."

I winced. I wouldn't have said it that way, but then again,

Kashvi wasn't exactly a newcomer. She could get away with a little more than I could.

Woody laughed until it turned into a coughing fit. When he caught his breath, he said, "Come by at three. Maybe I'll remember something new. Or maybe I need time to cover up the evidence of my crime."

The line went dead before either of us could say a word.

"You think he's joking?" I asked, staring at the phone.

Kashvi shrugged. "With that cough? He wouldn't make it halfway through an attack before he keeled over. But hey, we'll find out."

We moved on to Norma. Kashvi was careful not to say anything against the cops—Norma got there all on her own. She ranted for a solid minute about the uselessness of the new detectives before agreeing to meet with us later that afternoon.

Tina was more direct. She said she didn't know anything but was fine with a visit. Then she asked if we'd pick up her grocery order from Valdez's on the way. Kashvi agreed without hesitation, because of course she did.

We finished up around noon with a solid plan: Woody at three, Tina after, then Norma. Jet had his walking tour until one, so he'd join us unless something went wrong, like a twisted ankle or the van breaking down.

Kashvi started tidying up the back room while I gathered up the empty coffee cups and muffin wrappers.

"You sure you're okay with this?" she asked as I moved toward the door.

"Yeah," I said. "I'll meet you here later to head over to our first official investigating action."

18

Tina's groceries weren't ready.

Correction: Tina hadn't actually ordered them yet. So instead of a quick stop, we were in for a day of driving the outskirts of Nueva Vida.

On paper, the town was small. If you stuck close to the diner, you'd think it was just a quaint little downtown with a few attached neighborhoods, a school, a clinic, and one three-story business center. But outside of that? Nueva Vida was huge. Spread out. Sparse.

Seventy percent of the town's population lived scattered through the hills. Not quite wilderness, but not exactly paved streets and sidewalks, either. An obligatory Walmart sat beside a dusty little industrial area off the highway, but beyond that, the landscape was pure desert and scrub. Wide open and deceptively quiet.

Woody Howell lived in a 1950s rancher on a dirt street lined with seven identical, well-kept houses. Each had a mailbox out front and a gravel driveway leading to a parking space. No lawns. Out here, keeping grass alive wasn't worth the water. Most of the houses had given up on curb appeal, but Woody's place had two chainsaw-carved animal sculptures guarding the front yard—a bear and a coyote, both weather-worn but impressive.

He opened the door as we stepped out of the van, waiting while we made our way up the short walk.

"Don't get many visitors," he said, holding the door wide as we trooped inside. "Got tea, coffee, or water. Grab a seat. I'll be back."

The living room was a surprise. Immaculately kept, mid-century furniture, the upholstery spotless. The area rug was new. And his TV? A massive flat screen mounted on the wall beneath a satellite dish we'd noticed on the drive up.

"His place is nicer than mine," I murmured as I settled onto one end of the couch, not in a jealous way, but in a kind of I should be doing more with my home way.

"So," Woody said as he returned with a tray of drinks, "you want to know about the dead guy."

His hands trembled slightly, knuckles swollen and fingers bent with arthritis. I'd noticed that at the diner when he came in for an occasional Friday dinner special. Still, I couldn't help but wonder: Could he have held a knife firmly enough to kill?

I took an iced tea; Kashvi and Jet each chose water. Woody set the tray down on the kidney-shaped coffee table and eased into the recliner opposite us. His spine was curved from decades behind a desk, but there was still a rangy strength to him. Faded blue eyes studied us carefully.

"What did you tell the police?" Kashvi asked as she dug into her oversized purse. She pulled out a small glass jar and held it out to him. "I found an old recipe for aching joints. Rub that balm on and let me know if it helps."

Woody gave a crooked smile. "The old one you gave me

wasn't bad. Don't know if it worked or if the smell just made me think it did."

He popped open the jar, and a warm, earthy scent filled the room—herbs and spices, all familiar and soothing.

Kashvi had a thing for old remedies. Salves and ointments weren't a replacement for modern medicine, but they helped for the symptoms. And right now, they were helping Woody relax.

He closed the jar and set it aside.

"Told the cops it was a scam," he said. "Some kind of real estate thing. They wanted proof. Guess forty years as an accountant doesn't count for much when you're old."

"I'm happy to hear what your gut told you," Jet said, leaning forward. "We're not here to prove anything. Eliza got dragged into this because the guy had a receipt from her diner. We're just trying to clear her name so the cops can handle the arrest."

Woody gave me a brief nod. "I would hate to see your place close. Nowhere else in town makes cornbread worth a damn."

"Thank you," I said, keeping my expression polite. It was a compliment, but I wasn't ready to trust anyone just yet.

"He was a good con man," Woody went on. "Most folks around here are smart enough to spot a deal that's too good to be true. But he made it just good enough. Buy some land, hold onto it for a few years while a new development kicks off, then sell for a profit. Sounded reasonable."

"That's how legit developers operate," I said before I could stop myself. "They let their friends know early. It's not illegal, even if it's not fair. But you're saying there wasn't a development planned?"

Woody grinned. "Bingo. I checked while he was talking. Nothing online. No announcements, no zoning meetings,

no investment groups sniffing around. There's always something if a real project's coming. I gave all this to the cops, but
that young one—Detective Collett? She said all we had was
our guesses. They want hard evidence. You can imagine
how Norma took that."

I bit back a sharp comment about George and Denise's
bedside manner and focused on the condensation sliding
down my glass instead. I wasn't here to argue.

Not yet.

"I'll take the details," Kashvi said smoothly. "Maybe we
can find something he pulled in another town."

Woody nodded. "Tina Ingles was there. She told me you
were stopping by later and asked if she should talk to you."
He paused, thinking. "Norma Jackson, too. Don't know if the
cops got to her yet. Brad Vincent was there, and you ought
to talk to Betty Franks. I'll text you if I think of more. We all
go to the same meetings and socials—hard to keep track of
who was where sometimes."

I knew the feeling. If I had to recall which of my regulars
came into the diner on a specific day, I'd have to check the
receipts to be even close to sure.

"Some people were pretty desperate," he added. "Didn't
like it when I started asking questions. But I'm not about to
sit by and let some fast talker take advantage of folks."

Kashvi nodded, scribbling names in her notebook.
Woody handed her a neatly written note listing everything
he remembered about the so-called seminar.

"Don't you go investigating," Jet said as we stood to leave.
"We don't know if this killer's still around."

Woody's faded eyes twinkled. "Just as dangerous for you,
Michael. And for you two as well." His smile faded into
something serious. "I'll be careful. But I'll talk to a few
people. See if they remember anyone else listening in."

Jet had stiffened slightly at his real name. "Be careful," he repeated.

I wasn't sure if Woody was volunteering to help—or laying the groundwork to intimidate anyone else from talking. Either way, I mentally left his name on my list of maybe suspects. For now.

19

The grocery store texted me that Tina's order was finally ready. Perfect timing. Tina lived across town from Woody's house, and Norma probably wasn't home yet. At least we wouldn't be stuck waiting around before our next interview.

I knew murder cases didn't get solved overnight, despite what TV shows wanted us to believe. But every little delay gave the killer more time to get away—if they hadn't already.

We swung by Valdez's and picked up three bags of groceries before heading into the kind of neighborhood that sold the American dream. Older, well-kept houses lined the street, some still with white picket fences. They'd all started life as modest ranch homes, but most had been expanded over the years—garages, sunrooms, porches. The front yards were carefully designed with cactus and rock gardens instead of grass. Practical and pretty.

Tina didn't come out to greet us when we pulled up. Jet grabbed two of the bags and handed me the third. Kashvi was already halfway up the front walk.

As we got closer, the sound of Nina Simone drifted out through an open window—low and mournful. Not loud enough to annoy the neighbors, but louder than I expected for such a small house.

The door swung open before we knocked. A woman stood there, one hand on her hip, her scowl sharp enough to cut glass.

"I'm not turning it down, you—" Her expression froze mid-snap. "Oh. It's you."

Her scowl softened into something that might have passed for a smile on a less skeptical face. She stepped aside.

"Come in before my ice cream melts."

"Afternoon," Jet said, lifting the grocery bags in greeting. "Where do you want these?"

"Kitchen counter," Tina said, waving us toward the back of the house. "We can talk while I put this stuff away. Don't know if I've got anything to say, but it's your time to waste."

She led the way down a short hallway, her hands darting out here and there to straighten a photo frame or nudge an ornament into perfect alignment. Every surface was covered in china figurines and photos. It had to take hours to keep it this dust-free.

The kitchen was another story. Bright, open, and oddly minimal. No tchotchkes, no clutter. The space felt... intentional. A sharp contrast to the living room. The walls were painted a sunny yellow, and the curtains had a cheerful fruit pattern that didn't quite match Tina's acid green hair or the six piercings in each ear.

I knew she'd been a guidance counselor before she retired, but I hadn't expected this version of her. Maybe, like Kashvi had said, Tina was finally doing all the things she used to tell teenagers not to do.

"I talked to Woody," Tina said as she unpacked the bags

on the counter. She checked each item over like she was grading a final exam. A dented can of soup or bruised apple might be grounds for a failing grade.

When she was satisfied, she sorted the items into neat clusters—cupboard, fridge, freezer.

"Put the kettle on," she said, distracted, waving vaguely toward the stove. "Tea's in the canister. Coffee pods are in the tin. I'll take lemon ginger."

I stood, glad for something to do while Kashvi and Jet handled the conversation. The kettle must have just been used because it came to a boil in a moment rather than the couple of minutes I expected. I found the canister easily enough and pulled out the tea bags, letting them steep while Tina kept sorting.

Once the last item was put away, she joined Kashvi and Jet at the vintage chrome-and-Formica kitchen table. She didn't sit so much as arrange herself, like she was posing for an old-school portrait.

"He said Brad and Betty were at the seminar," Tina said, getting right to the point. "I remember a few others, but I'm not handing out names if you're just going to sic the police on them. They were desperate, not criminals."

Good information. If only a few people had stayed, and we thought the scam was the motive—or revenge for a scam gone wrong—then a shorter list worked in our favor.

"Who stayed?" Jet asked. His voice was calm, coaxing. "We're just trying to move things along before this becomes something worse. None of us want this hanging over Nueva Vida."

"Well, someone sure does," Tina said, arching a brow. "Whoever did it'll be happy to let this go cold."

I poured the tea into our mugs and carried everything to

the table. We all opted for tea—maybe we'd hit our caffeine quota already.

"We think the cops need help," Kashvi said. "They don't know who's important to talk to yet."

"You mean who's nosy," Tina said, her mouth twitching like she was trying not to smile. "No offense taken. There's not much else to do around here but get into everyone's business." She glanced out the window at her tidy, paved backyard. "As long as I keep my judgments to myself, I figure I'm safe."

She took a sip of her tea, then looked back at us.

"Go talk to Norma. She'll have more to say. But if you want my opinion, the two people with the most to lose— and the most gullible—are Emily Stonehouse and Brad Vincent. You remember Emily, don't you, Jet? Always chasing the next big money-making scheme."

Jet nodded. "I remember."

"I've been trying to come up with other names while I waited for you," Tina said. "Nothing else yet. But it'll come."

I got the sense this was a test. Woody had set one, too. Maybe they were both seeing how we handled ourselves before they told us everything they knew.

"No suspects yet," Jet said. "We're not looking to confront anyone. Just following the clues."

"Good," Tina said, giving him a long look. "Because this isn't TV. The killer doesn't confess after two questions."

I set my mug down and glanced at the clock. Norma would be expecting us soon. I had a feeling Tina was enjoying the company more than she was interested in helping the investigation.

"You've made something of yourself," Tina said to Jet, her tone shifting to something almost warm. "Didn't think you'd ever straighten up. I'm proud of you."

Jet laughed. "Pretty sure 'tour guide' wasn't on your list of career options."

"You're making a living doing something you love," Tina said, lifting her cup in a small toast. "That's success in my book." She stared out the window for a moment. "I've seen too many of my students chase the dollars and hate their lives. You're a win. Not many of those in my past."

I'd never thought about success like that before. I'd always loved my work—maybe I was luckier than I realized. Jet might stick with guiding tours, or he might open his own business one day. Maybe he'd write books. His boundaries were his to choose. I liked that about him.

Then Tina turned to me, pulling me out of my thoughts. "You hired Will Strong."

It took me a second to switch gears. "He's doing a good job," I said carefully.

Tina's gaze sharpened, but not in a hostile way. "I knew he'd settle. Most kids who go through what he did... they don't. His mother saved him. Marrying Alan Strong gave that boy a chance."

She gave me a nod that felt like initiation into a club I hadn't applied to join. It wasn't unwelcome. If Tina was in your corner, you'd probably want to keep her there.

I wasn't sure if I was relieved or worried that she didn't seem like the kind of person who'd stab someone over a real estate scam. Then again, would she kill to protect someone she cared about? Someone who'd been taken in by Peter Trent?

"You get along now," Tina said as she stood, as if she'd decided we were done. "Thanks for the delivery. Good luck on the case."

And just like that, we were out the door and heading to Norma's.

20

On the way to Norma Jackson's house, I let my mind wander through everything we'd gathered so far.

Small-town life wasn't just different from what I was used to—it was almost a different language. The slower pace, the friendlier people. And underneath all that niceness was a steady current of curiosity that could feel downright intrusive. I'd had very little to do with Woody or Tina before today, but they already knew a lot about me. I wasn't part of their hidden grapevine, but I was clearly a topic.

I supposed participation came with time. And maybe trust. So far, all the talk about me seemed positive, which was good for business—and maybe even my social life. If I ever found time for one.

"Why are they being so helpful?" I asked, mostly to Kashvi. She was only a handful of years ahead of me here, and somehow no one treated her like an outsider. If I was going to fit in, I needed to understand how she'd done it.

"Me?" Jet answered before she could speak. He swung

the van around a tight corner with one hand on the wheel like he'd been born driving these roads.

"I've lived here my whole life. People know who I am, even when they don't think they do. Tina knows I'm not going to take advantage of anyone. But the flip side is, some of the old-timers can't see that I've grown up."

"It's nice to have that history," Kashvi said, twisting in her seat to look at him. "I guess I got a little lucky. Enough people here like to read, and without a public library, my lending section's the only option for a lot of them."

"Is the diner enough for me?" I asked. "As long as people like the food?"

Kashvi exchanged a look with Jet. He kept his gaze fixed on the road, which was probably the equivalent of a 'you tell her' in their silent language.

"Here's the thing," Kashvi said, her voice gentle. "You might be reading 'outsider' into people's words when they don't mean it that way. But... yeah. You need at least three people to sign off before anyone here stops seeing you as a stranger."

"Sign off?" I asked. "What, like an application process?"

"Sort of," she said, smiling. "It's not about whether they like you. That comes later. It's about deciding you belong."

I let that sit for a second. "So who's decided I belong?" Not just picking a side?

"Mrs. Waverly," Kashvi said. "She loves you for what you've done with the diner. Her father ran it, you know. She saw the decline under the last owner, and now it's back to what it was."

I blinked. I'd never even heard Mrs. Waverly say hello. She grunted, sometimes, and stared at me like she was figuring out whether I was compost or a tomato plant. And it sounded like the diner had been around a lot longer than I thought. "Okay... who else?"

"Woody," Jet said simply.

That one made sense. If Woody Howell was a community gatekeeper—and after today, I thought he might be—that approval was worth something.

"And Lola," Kashvi added. "Maybe even Jacquie. You gave them both jobs and trusted them to run things their way. Lola's a bit of a celebrity because of her books. And Jacquie? She's probably helped half the town at least once. You're in. Now it's about making an effort."

I let out a breath in one long swoosh. "Yes, ma'am," I said, smiling despite myself. I'd been building this whole story in my head about being excluded—and here I was, smack in the middle of things. "I guess I thought I was doing a good job making connections."

"You are," Kashvi said. "But now it's time for you to go deeper."

"Since we're on the topic," I said, "why is everyone so sure George and Denise can't solve this case? It can't all be about them coming from outside." A flash of pity went through me as I said it. How were they supposed to succeed if no one trusted them?

Jet slowed as we approached a quiet residential street.

"We're almost there," he said. "But you should hear it before we talk to Norma. If she senses you're not up to date, she'll make sure to educate you."

Kashvi twisted again to face me, her expression serious now.

"The short version? People don't think the cops have their priorities straight. George and Denise came from Santa Fe. That makes them big city, in our world. They're focused on shutting down the Devil Dogs, but to most folks here, those kids aren't criminals yet. They're neighbors' kids, or grandkids. No one wants them locked up. They think there's still a chance to turn them around."

I nodded slowly. Now that I knew what the gang was up to—and what they could become—it was hard to argue with George's strategy. But I also understood why the town wasn't ready to give up on them.

"What do people want instead?" I asked. "If not jail?"

"A few want them doing community service," Jet said. He pulled into a neighborhood that could have been anywhere. Stucco in earthy tones. Paved driveway. Two-car garage. Fake shutters on the windows. Neat. Impersonal.

"Restorative justice," Kashvi added. "We haven't agreed on a solution yet, but we'll get there."

Maybe that was my way in. Help the town come to an agreement. Lead a committee, maybe. I wasn't sure I wanted that job, but I did want to help keep Nueva Vida from turning into something dark.

Before I could follow that thought further, Jet cut the engine.

"We're here," he said. His voice was quieter now. More thoughtful.

Norma Jackson's house was unassuming. Tidy to the point of perfection. Yard mostly the local red-brown gravel with a path of flat round stones. The shutters were painted the exact shade of beige as the stucco, and the curtains behind them were closed. No garden gnomes. No welcome mat. Nothing out of place.

I stared at the house for a second longer than I meant to. Something about it put me on edge.

"She's going to test you," Kashvi warned softly. "Don't fail."

I straightened my shoulders and followed them up the walk.

And for the first time since we'd started this investigation, I found myself wondering if we were about to talk to a killer.

21

"You're late," Norma said as she ushered us inside. Her voice was brisk, but not rude. She was in her late fifties—if appearances could be trusted. Short gray hair, sharp as steel wool, jeans, and a faded Grateful Dead Final Tour 1995 t-shirt. Worn, but clearly cared for. The sort of thing you held onto because it carried memories.

I followed Kashvi and Jet into the living room, where the walls were covered in framed photos. Most of them showed Norma at concerts, usually with another woman. They were close. Very close. It was obvious in the way they smiled at each other—genuine joy captured again and again.

Kashvi bumped my elbow as I stared a second too long. She leaned in just enough to whisper, "That's Rose. They got married as soon as the law passed. Had ten good years. Rose died of cancer. Fast."

I nodded. That was more than enough to understand why Norma didn't like talking about it. And why we wouldn't bring it up.

"Sit," Norma said, pointing us toward the kitchen. "I've

got iced tea and lemonade. Too late in the day for caffeine." She raised an eyebrow. "Yes, I know tea has caffeine. It doesn't bother my sleep."

Her tone made me think we weren't the first people to challenge her beverage choices. She carried two pitchers to the table and set down four tall glasses, each with a single ice cube.

"Serve yourselves," she said. "Then tell me what you want. I don't have much time to waste."

The kitchen was larger than I expected. Open. Clean. Too clean, maybe. The table sat in a nook, built-in seating on three sides—Jet nudged me in first and slid in next to me. Trapped. Kashvi took the seat opposite. Norma sat in an old wooden chair at the open end, like the captain of a ship.

I poured a little lemonade into my glass and took a slow sip, watching her. I didn't have any special skill at reading people, but something about Norma put me on alert. Maybe it was her precision. Everything about her was neat, organized. Controlled. And yet... I'd seen the faint shine in her eyes when she glanced at Rose's photos.

"Woody told us you were at the seminar," Jet said. "The one where Peter Trent tried to scam people out of their money."

Norma's mouth tightened. For a second, I thought she might tell Jet to leave. Instead, she sighed through her nose and tapped a short rhythm on the table with her fingers.

"Did you notice anything that might point to the killer?" I asked, keeping my tone easy. Friendly. "Or even a suspect?"

"What exactly did Woody tell you?" she asked, her gaze sharp. "He can get up on his high horse fast. I'm not about to point fingers on my word alone."

So no love lost there. But there was respect. It was clear in the way she said his name—biting, but not dismissive.

"That you were there," Kashvi said smoothly. "With Tina Ingles. A few others. It wasn't that long ago, so we thought you might remember more people. The official investigation's moving slow, so we're hoping to help it along. Make sure the detectives know who's not a suspect."

Norma took a drink before she answered.

"I'm not losing my memory like that old goat. Tina was her usual pushy self that night. But I guess this time, she was right. Pegged him as a crook just before it hit me."

Her voice dropped slightly on that last sentence, her fingers still drumming. Something wasn't sitting right.

And then it clicked. Norma had almost fallen for it.

"You were thinking about investing," I said. I wasn't accusing her, just stating a fact I could feel in my gut.

Norma looked at me. Really looked at me. For a heartbeat, I thought she was about to kick me out.

Then she rubbed a hand over her eyes, not quite fast enough to hide the moisture there.

"I'm usually smarter than that," she said quietly. "But... I didn't realize how much I still missed Rose. She always wanted to travel. We never had enough money to go far. And for a minute, I thought if I invested in his scheme, maybe I could finally go. Maybe she'd be along for the ride. In spirit."

Her words hung there, heavy and raw.

Grief's a sneaky thing. Even when you think you've packed it away, it finds you. I hadn't loved Joseph by the time he died—he'd made sure of that. But for months after, I'd still find myself reaching for his favorite cookies in the store. Forgetting. Remembering. Grief messes with you, whether you welcome it or not.

"But you realized," I said gently. "And pulled back."

Norma nodded. "Woody and Tina scared most people

off. I woke up a few myself. That Peter guy... he looked like he wanted to spit nails."

She laughed, but it was bitter. "As far as I know, he didn't get anyone to sign on the dotted line." The way she said it made me wonder. Was she sure? Or was she hoping?

Jet cleared his throat. "We think someone might have invested. And then changed their mind."

Norma tilted her head. "That'd make sense," she admitted. "I noticed two people who didn't seem to hear the warnings. Emily Stonehouse. And Brad Vincent."

I glanced at Jet. The second time these two were mentioned. So we had two suspects. Or at least, two people with motive. We still didn't know for sure the murder was about the scam, but it was something to follow.

"Where was the seminar held?" I asked, realizing how little we'd asked about the event. "Any paperwork involved?"

"The Lions Club rented him a room," Norma said. "They don't screen people holding meetings."

I made a mental note to check into that. A paper trail might be the only trail we got.

Norma stared past me toward the backyard, her expression distant. "There's something," she murmured. "I know I'm forgetting something important. But you know how it is. The harder you chase a memory, the faster it runs."

I did know. And I also knew she was holding something back. Maybe not the thing that would solve this case. Maybe something else entirely. But the way her shoulders tensed as she spoke... Norma had a secret. And I wasn't sure if it was connected to Peter Trent, or something much bigger.

My stomach rumbled, loud enough to make Kashvi snort. I laughed, embarrassed, and pushed back my glass.

"We should go. Dinner at Los Amigos. Want to join us?"

I wasn't sure where the offer came from. Pity? Maybe. Or

maybe it was what Kashvi would call building community. Reaching out.

Norma gave me a long look. Then—surprisingly— smiled. "Thanks for the offer," she said. "But I was up at dawn. I'll be heading to bed soon."

She stood, and so did we.

"Maybe my mind will work it out while I sleep," she added.

I hoped so. Because whatever she was holding on to, it was starting to feel important. And I wasn't sure how long we had left before this case turned cold.

22

L os Amigos sat on the edge of town, close enough to the highway to catch tourists looking for a quick meal. It wasn't exactly right next to the off-ramp, but it was close enough.

The food was fresh, the tortillas were handmade, and the beer was cold. Not that we were planning to drink—Jet had to drive, and all of us needed to keep our heads clear. But the most important thing? The aroma.

Mexican spices hung in the air, warm and inviting. A restaurant should always smell like what they cooked that day. At EB Eats, it was bacon in the morning and whatever was on the grill by lunch. At night, the faint scent of disinfectant lingered, but the key was keeping it all fresh. Clean. No build-up of grease.

Los Amigos got it right. And tonight, we needed that comfort food to keep us going.

We placed our orders and settled into a corner booth by the front window, a little separated from the rest of the dining room. The place was nearly full, a low hum of conversation and clinking silverware surrounding us. If we kept our voices down, we could talk about the case without drawing attention.

After drinks arrived—cola for Jet, horchatas for Kashvi and me—we pulled out our murder books.

"I think this is the first time we've had something to write that might be an actual clue," I said.

The waitress brought our food just then—our favorite, enchiladas all around and a fresh bowl of salsa. I leaned back to give her room, then offered a thank you.

She smiled. "Anything else you need?"

"We're good," I said, and she moved on to the next table.

The plates were hot, steam rising from the melted cheese. I wanted to dig in, but I also didn't want to burn the roof of my mouth. Kashvi cut into hers and winced at the heat.

"It's hard to wait," I said, grabbing a chip and scooping up some salsa to distract myself.

Jet was already jotting things down in his notebook.

"I got a text," he said. "Woody sent a couple more names. Steve Gordon, Greg Everett, and Tommy Bullsmith. That makes six people to talk to."

"Progress," Kashvi said.

"Let's eat," Jet added.

Between bites of salad and rice, we kept tossing ideas around. Kashvi was halfway through her enchilada when Jet said, "We can call the Lions Club. Alf Dooken's the secretary, right?"

Kashvi groaned. "Don't make me call him. Please."

I raised an eyebrow. "Why not?"

She stabbed at her rice. "The only way to discourage his matchmaking is to avoid him."

I blinked. "Wait. Aren't you and Jet...?" I let the question hang.

"She thought that would buy her immunity," Jet said, grinning. "He's not convinced."

"He keeps trying to set me up with nephews and distant cousins," Kashvi muttered. "If he had kids of his own, I'm sure he'd be dragging them in too."

I laughed, the warmth of it loosening something in my chest. "I've had my share of matchmakers. Even friends try to do it." I gave her a pretend stern look. "Let me call. I don't remember Alf as a customer. Maybe he'll focus on answering my questions and leave my love life out of it."

Jet gave me a mock salute. "Brave woman."

I found the number online and checked the contact hours. Five minutes left.

When a man answered, I went with friendly.

"Hi, I'm looking into a booking. You have an event room, right?"

"I can help you with that," Alf said. His voice was brisk. Businesslike. Not exactly warm. "What day were you thinking?"

"I'm actually hoping you can tell me something about the man who held the real estate seminar a few days ago?"

There was a beat of silence.

"The murdered guy?"

"Peter Trent," I confirmed. "Did he leave contact information?"

"I already gave all that to the detectives," Alf said. "Why should I tell you?"

I took a breath. He wasn't going to make this easy.

"I'm Eliza Burton. I own EB Eats." I paused. "You've probably heard of us."

"I know the place," he said. "Alf, by the way. Still don't see why I should tell you."

Grump.

I resisted the urge to roll my eyes at my friends, but realized they couldn't hear Alf, so there was no point.

"Some of the people I've met lately are getting impatient," I said. "They want this over. If I can help, it's worth asking."

More silence. I set the phone between my shoulder and ear and cut into my enchilada. It had cooled enough to eat, but I didn't want to be rude.

"They do seem to be dragging their feet," Alf said finally. "You married?"

"Divorced," I said, deadpan. "And a little too busy to change that."

Kashvi nearly spit out her horchata. Jet snorted and returned to mixing his rice into his refried beans.

"Hmm," Alf said. "Well, I told that detective woman I checked his registration as soon as I heard about the murder. The address he gave doesn't exist, and the phone number's out of service."

Disappointing, but not surprising. "Anything else?"

"He had a partner," Alf said. "Didn't see her. But I heard him tell her to get him a coffee while he was on the phone. She didn't sound pleased."

I sat up straighter. A partner? That was new. "Did you tell the police?" I asked.

"They didn't ask," Alf said. "We're closing now. You let me know when you're ready to date. I've got a whole gang of relatives, and they were all brought up right."

The call ended before I could think of a polite exit.

I put the phone down and picked up my fork instead. I wasn't explaining until I'd eaten something. Kashvi and Jet were still grinning.

"So?" Jet asked after I finished half my plate.

I made them wait another bite. Maybe two.

Then I relented.

"Contact information was bogus. Denise knows that already. But Alf mentioned something else." I glanced between them. "Peter Trent had a partner. Female. Alf didn't see her, but he heard them talking."

Kashvi leaned forward. "And the cops don't know?"

"Denise didn't ask the right question," I said. It wasn't a good reason to withhold the information, but the petty side of me relished the proof we were gathering intel the cops missed.

They both sat back, processing.

"We've got a lot to do tomorrow," Jet said after a beat. "What's your shift?"

"I'm opening," I said. "I'm free after noon."

"I can get Mallory to cover me," Kashvi said. "Jet?"

"I'm in the office. I'll set up the interviews. Meet at five when I'm done?"

"Sounds good," I said.

We polished off the rest of our food in companionable silence, the conversation circling in my head.

A partner.

That changed things.

A lot.

23

"I have something to show you," Kashvi said as we paid the bill. "And don't argue—it's too soon to go home after eating. You're supposed to wait before bed. Or maybe that's swimming?"

"It's both," I said. "But I'd rather hang out than do housework."

And truthfully? I wasn't quite ready to be alone with my thoughts. "What is it?"

"You'll see." She gave me a grin.

"Jet, can you keep the van? Drive Eliza home after, so she won't be too energized from the walk to sleep?"

He agreed. I didn't argue. A ride home sounded better than walking, even if the bookstore was only a few blocks away.

Jet slid behind the wheel but didn't start the van right away.

"I've been thinking," he said. "We should tell George and Denise what we've found. Not everything, but some of it. Like the partner. That's important."

I stiffened. "We can tell them... when we know more," I

said, choosing each word carefully. "If we hand things over now, George will just tell us to stop butting in. That's how he says 'thank you'—by shutting us down." I paused, then added, "And it's late. I'm sure he's not available."

"Ooh," Kashvi said, leaning in to waggle her eyebrows at Jet.

"Afraid to see him? Maybe you'll end up liking him if you get to know him. I bet it's lonely, being new in town and arresting people for a living."

"I thought you didn't like matchmakers," I said, aiming a mock glare in her direction. "Want me to tell Alf you're interested?"

She gave me a cheeky smile and held up a hand. "I don't like people matchmaking me, because I'm with Jet. But you're single."

I opened my mouth to argue. Closed it. Opened it again.

Nothing came out that didn't sound petty in my head.

Kashvi nodded knowingly. "And I agree with Jet. We've found something important. If people are withholding facts because they don't think George and Denise can solve the case, then we need to fix that."

"Fine, I'll call him," I said. I reached for my phone, sighing. "I'll do it when we get to the bookstore. He can meet us at The Open Page, or I'll leave a message to come by the diner tomorrow."

Jet started the van. "Call now. Might as well get it over with."

I sent up a quick wish that George wouldn't answer. I needed more time to figure out what to tell him—and maybe get something back from him in return. It wasn't like we were interfering, right? We hadn't poked around the crime scene. Yet.

No such luck.

"Kramer." He didn't even say hello. Was this a seventies cop show?

"It's Eliza Burton," I said. "I have some information for you. Can you come to The Open Page in ten minutes?"

"Tell me over the phone," he said, all business.

"Not happening," I replied. "I'm on my way there now. You can meet us in person, or I'll leave a message for you at the diner tomorrow."

Offer a choice. My old negotiating tactic. Worked on toddlers, bosses, and apparently detectives.

There was a pause. Then, "See you in fifteen." The call ended, abrupt as always.

Jet parked in front of the bookstore. Kashvi hopped out, digging through her purse for the keys.

"Hang on," she said over her shoulder. "Alarm first."

She disappeared inside, and within seconds the familiar beep stopped. Lights flicked on—just the seating area up front and the back room.

I dropped into the closest chair with a sigh and set my purse down next to me. "So. What are we telling him?"

"Definitely the partner," Jet said. He remained standing, facing the door. Probably so George couldn't sneak up on us. I appreciated the thought.

"And the names?" I asked as Kashvi reappeared and slid into a chair opposite me. "Do we hand over the list from Woody, Tina, and Norma?"

Kashvi's lips thinned. "I'm not sure we should violate their trust. We promised nothing, but still... I'll leave that to you two."

And before we could argue, she stood. "I've got things to do in the back. Come find me when he's gone."

Jet and I exchanged looks as she disappeared.

"Why does it feel like she just abandoned us?" I asked.

"Because she did," Jet said with a faint grin. He stayed standing. "And when did we promise confidentiality?"

"We didn't." I sighed. "But I think they told us things knowing we'd pass it on to the cops—without having to get involved themselves."

"I'm okay being the middleman," Jet said. "As long as George doesn't think we're holding out on him."

"I'm okay being the middlewoman, I guess." I looked toward the door. "But I'm not handing over everything. I need this case solved before people start thinking it's too dangerous to eat at my diner."

"He's here," Jet said, nodding toward the door as George Kramer walked in.

His gaze swept the bookstore, then settled on me. And suddenly, it was very clear who was expected to do the talking.

24

G eorge wasn't alone.

Denise Collett stepped into the bookstore ahead of him and took the chair next to mine. George stayed back, leaning against a bookshelf, arms crossed like he didn't plan on sitting. They both looked exhausted. Pale, tight around the eyes. The kind of tired that comes from chasing something hard and not quite catching it.

I didn't mention it. I'd been there myself—days spent testing recipes, grabbing cat naps, getting annoyed when someone told me to stop. Both of them were professionals. They knew their limits. They didn't need me pointing them out.

What they did need was information. I wasn't about to waste their time explaining why we were still investigating.

"We've talked to a few people," I began. "I know you have too, but sometimes folks are reluctant to talk to the authorities. Scared they'll get it wrong. And if that happens, if you arrest the wrong person on a neighbor's tip? Well, it's not something people forget."

Denise's jaw clenched, but she said nothing.

"Don't worry about it," George said, his tone mild. "We're following up on our interviews tomorrow. If you saved us some time, that's a benefit." His gaze flicked to Denise, like he was reminding her to stay calm.

Or maybe I was reading into it. I was starting to see why people found small towns exhausting.

Jet stayed quiet, arms folded. I couldn't tell if he was holding back or just letting me lead. Either way, I was fine with sticking to facts.

"One thing you might not know," I said, "Peter Trent had a partner. A woman."

"In the real estate scam?" Denise leaned in, suddenly sharp. "Who is she?"

Was he running more than one con?

"Yes, the real estate scam," I confirmed. "I don't know who she is. Alf Dooken overheard him speaking to her. You should follow up with him."

Denise's eyes narrowed. "How sure are you that Alf's not making a bid for attention?"

Her voice was clipped. Too clipped. She was holding herself together by sheer will. Trying to prove something.

Jet spoke before I could. "Alf doesn't want attention. He's too busy matchmaking his extended family to make things up. You do know his reputation is about his misguided attempts to marry off his cousins, right?" He let that hang for a second. "Or don't you know anything about the people who live here?"

I winced, waiting for the blowback.

But George nodded instead, like Jet had made a fair point.

When Denise opened her mouth to argue, he cut her off with a look. It wasn't harsh. Just firm. A reminder.

George shifted, pulling out a small notebook. "What else have you learned?"

"A few names. People who were at the seminar," I said. "But I don't think Peter managed to scam anyone before... well, before he ended up dead."

"We already have the list of attendees," Denise said, her tone flat.

"Then I guess the partner is all we had to offer," I replied.

In my head, it sounded fine. In my ears, I heard the edge of petulance.

"Okay," George said as he closed his notebook. "Thanks for that." He gave me a tired smile. "Now, you really need to leave the rest to the professionals. We may not know the community like you three do—yes, I know Kashvi's lurking back there—but we know our jobs." He tilted his head slightly. "Would you like it if I came into your kitchen and started slinging hash?"

His smile softened the words, tired though it was. There was warmth behind it. Or maybe just an attempt at diplomacy.

"If you can cook, maybe I'd be fine," I said, smiling back. "But I don't think you want to step into Jacquie's domain."

George chuckled, low and dry. For a second, I wondered what he was like when he wasn't running on fumes.

Denise wasn't laughing. She rose and took a step toward me. "Knowing how to fry an egg is not the same as police work," she snapped. "We know how to interrogate someone. We carry guns if things go sideways." Her jaw was tight enough to crack. "So stop interfering."

George closed his eyes for half a second. Shook his head, just once. I got the feeling that training Denise was usually his job, and right now, he didn't have the energy. Or maybe this was deliberate—good cop, bad cop, both of them tired enough to make it believable.

I wasn't sure which thought I liked better. Still, I tried one more time. "Have you made any progress? Any suspects?"

Denise answered automatically. "We don't discuss ongoing investigations." She could have been reading from a script. There wasn't a drop of feeling in it.

"Detective Collett is right," George said, shooting her a glance that clearly meant ease up. "But maybe this will help convince you to stop." He pocketed his notebook and pushed off the bookcase. "We found the murder weapon. In a trash bin. No prints."

That got my attention. I opened my mouth to ask where, but George was already turning away.

"Now we're getting some rest," he said.

Denise was right behind him.

"Fine," she said, not looking at us. "See you at eight, at the station."

They were gone before I could ask whether that invitation included us.

25

I glanced at Jet once George and Denise were gone. "What was that?"

Jet's brow furrowed. "What was what?"

"That whole... thing," I said, waving vaguely toward the door. "He wants our information, but he doesn't want us gathering it?"

Jet exhaled slowly, rubbing the back of his neck. "I'm not sure he knows how to react around Denise. You didn't see his face when she started in on you. I did—and I've seen it before. He's annoyed at her attitude, but he's too tired to deal with it properly."

That was fair. Exhaustion made it hard to keep your temper in check—or someone else's. But still. "She's an adult," I said. "A cranky one, sure, but she's responsible for her behavior. I'm not sure how I feel about George... handling her."

Jet glanced at me. "Handling?"

"You know what I mean." I sighed. "I'd like him to, because I'm tired of taking the brunt of her dislike. But the idea of a man 'handling' a woman? It's not feminism—it's just basic respect. She's not his problem to fix."

Jet gave a small shrug. "Training's a wide range of tactics. Number one is don't criticize in public. I've had tour guides who wouldn't learn, no matter what I tried. We only see Denise now and then. George knows her better. Maybe he understands what she needs to display to be successful."

I wasn't convinced, but I let it go. I was too tired to untangle the difference between support and control.

"Come on," I said. "Kashvi wants us in the back. Let's see what her big surprise is."

Jet headed toward the closed door. "I have no idea when she found time to put anything together. We've been running ourselves ragged."

My curiosity overrode the weariness dragging at my limbs. I followed close behind him—and bumped into his back when he came to a sudden, complete stop.

"What the heck, Jet?" I muttered.

He shifted to the side with an apologetic grin and pointed. "Look."

Kashvi stood by the far wall like a proud game show hostess, her hands sweeping toward what she clearly considered her prize.

Not a puzzle. Not a bookshelf.

A murder board.

Red string. Photos. Printouts. Peter Trent's face at the center of a web of connections, with lines stretching out toward everyone we'd talked to—and some we hadn't. A bright pink paper labeled with a bold black question mark represented the mystery partner.

I stood there, momentarily speechless. Then I shut my mouth, walked forward, and took it all in. "You did this... today?" I asked.

"This morning," Kashvi said, smiling wide. "I figured we needed a bigger picture. It helps, right?"

"Helps?" I shook my head in disbelief. "This is amazing. It must have taken you hours."

She laughed. "Not really. Just an hour or two. Mostly it was printing photos. And I didn't want to jam a whiteboard in here—this wall works just fine."

"And you updated it while we were talking to the detectives," Jet added, his admiration clear. "Makes me feel like we're actual professionals."

"The only thing I didn't do," Kashvi said, "was write up a list of the questions we still need to ask. I'm not about to write directly on the wall, so we'll need a list I can print."

She waved us toward the table. Her laptop was already open and waiting.

I gave the board one more glance before sitting. "If we were professionals, and this was permanent, I know a product to paint on the wall so we could wipe it clean later."

Kashvi snorted. "Don't tempt me."

"But we're not," I said. "We won't need this again."

Right?

"We'll leave investigations to the professionals... after this."

Jet raised an eyebrow. "Sure we will."

I didn't argue. Not because I agreed, but because it was easier to keep moving.

"Let's start with the interviews tomorrow," Kashvi said, fingers poised over the keyboard. "What does our board tell us we need to know?"

In fifteen minutes, we had a list of pointed questions and another list of action items.

I had no illusions about how realistic this was—I'm sure it's only on TV cop shows that murder boards stand in public view. But there was something powerful about seeing the connections mapped out in red string. I found myself hoping one of those lines pointed straight to the killer.

"You need sleep," Jet told Kashvi, his tone gentle but brooking no argument.

I felt a tiny pang of jealousy. Not about Jet. About the fact someone was making sure she took care of herself. Not that I needed anyone to tell me to get some rest. I'm fine.

"I'll call and set up the interviews," I offered, brushing the thought aside. "Half an hour each, with travel time. If we stay on schedule, we'll be done by dinner."

"I can do it," Jet said. "But I'm happy to leave it to you, if it makes you feel useful." He dodged my poke at his arm for the joking patronizing.

"My treat at the diner," I said. "After."

We agreed: Brad Vincent, Emily Stonehouse, and Betty Franks were the priorities. They'd come up more than once in our conversations. If we found anything new, we'd move on to Greg Everett, Steve Gordon, and Tommy Bullsmith.

By the time we wrapped up, I was yawning.

Ten minutes later, I stood in my driveway, waving as Jet and Kashvi drove away. Then I turned toward the house, bracing myself for the mess waiting inside.

The living room was untidy but not terrible. No mugs growing mold. No plates crusted with ancient crumbs. It was never as bad as I expected. Maybe Macchiato didn't feel the need to punish me for staying out all day. And, I guessed all those diner habits were sticking—clean as you go.

I decided I could live with a little mess for now. The case needed my attention more than dust bunnies did.

Still... maybe it was time to hire a cleaner. I'd think about it when I wasn't bone-tired.

I dropped my purse on the coffee table and headed for bed.

Four hours of sleep would have to be enough.

26

Between morning customers, I managed to contact two people on our list of... what?

Suspects?

I wasn't ready to go there. Not yet.

Breakfast service ran smoothly. Most of my regulars turned up, more interested in gossip than eggs or pancakes. I hated to think the murder was good for business, but here we were. The lull came around ten-thirty. Half the tables were empty, and I was about to start prepping for lunch when the front door slammed open.

Alistair.

He came in like a desert storm, face red, eyes wide. "You're trying to frame me!" he shouted, pointing directly at me.

Every conversation stopped. Forks froze halfway to mouths. Chairs creaked as people twisted in their seats to get a better view of the drama. It wasn't every day entertainment came with coffee refills.

I sighed quietly and stepped out from behind the counter. "What are you talking about?"

I kept my voice even, calm. I really wanted to kick him out, but that would only make it worse. You didn't throw gasoline on a wildfire.

He marched up to me, all puffed-up outrage. "You put the murder weapon in the trash behind my restaurant!" he said, jabbing a finger at the air between us. "You killed that man," he hissed, "and now you want to destroy me. A well-respected member of the community!"

From the back booth, someone snorted. Loudly. I didn't have to look to know it was Katie Wise.

"I did no such thing," I said, taking a slow step forward.

His eyes flickered. Real fear there, under the bluster.

"I'm sure the police will do their diligence," I added. "If you're innocent, you have nothing to worry about."

"Of course I'm innocent," he snapped. He straightened, smoothing his shirt like he could iron out his temper. Then he jabbed a finger toward my shoulder.

I sidestepped, and he stumbled a little, losing momentum. "You'll regret this," he growled. "I have plenty I can tell the police about you."

With that, he spun on his heel and stormed out the door, nearly knocking over Mr. Gonzalez on the way.

The diner stayed silent for a beat.

Then Katie spoke up. "He's full of hot air," she said. "I guess the real killer just dumped the weapon. Too bad. We could all use a break from Alistair. I'm not saying he should go to prison, but a couple of days in holding would be a relief."

A ripple of chuckles followed.

I was tempted to join in, but Kashvi's advice floated back —you have to take sides to fit in. I didn't think she meant now.

"I'd be scared too if it was my trash bin," I said instead,

wiping my hands on a towel. "He'll cool down." I caught a few approving nods. "I'm pretty sure he's not the killer," I added, pitching my voice lighter. "And I know I'm not."

I gave a little mock bow, which earned me a few laughs.

"Now," I said, heading back to the counter, "who wants a coffee top-up?"

Almost every hand in the room lifted.

Business as usual.

For now.

27

By the time I headed to the bookstore to meet Kashvi, I'd tried Brad Vincent ten times, left three messages. No response. It wasn't like I was ready to label him a suspect. Not yet. But the silence had me thinking things I didn't like.

I found Jet and Kashvi already deep in conversation. As soon as I sat down, I told them about Alistair's latest performance at the diner.

"Oh, we heard," Kashvi said, rolling her eyes. "By the time you headed here, half the town had their own version of the story rolling out. Everyone knows what he's like. He's his own worst enemy. But he still has plenty of people eating at Dunes—even if he's serving food from the fifties."

I wasn't worried about Alistair. Not exactly. But there'd been a flicker of fear in his eyes that didn't sit right with me.

"Do you think he might have invested in Trent's scheme?" I asked. "He was scared of something—I'm pretty sure it wasn't me. And he visited the man before the seminar."

Kashvi shrugged, adding Alistair's name to the murder board.

"If they found the weapon behind Dunes," she said, "George and Denise will be all over him."

"Which means we leave Alistair to them and go to Brad first," Jet said, pulling the van out of the parking space as soon as he heard our seatbelts click. "Not just because we want to talk to him. He's an old man who lives alone. Not answering his phone could mean he's hurt."

That had been eating at me all morning. "Does he have family?"

"A nephew," Kashvi said. "Vic Vincent. He's here in Nueva Vida. Brad's got family scattered all over the state, but Vic is the only one who checks on him."

I nodded but couldn't shake the tightness in my chest. "And you're sure he's fine?"

Kashvi glanced over her shoulder. "We'll know soon. But Vic made him get one of those fall alarms, so if something had happened, he'd already have help."

The reassurance helped. A little.

We drove farther out of town, past the usual scattering of homes. This was what my friends back in Oregon would have called the bush—lonely stretches of scrub and dirt, nothing but sky and the occasional fence to remind you someone lived out here.

Brad's house sat at the end of a long gravel road. Solid structure. Fenced yard. And that was about where the good points ended.

When we opened the gate and started up the path to the front door, Brad Vincent stepped out with a shotgun.

"Get off my land!" he barked.

No shaky hands. No hesitation. He held that weapon like a man who'd spent his life hunting. His skin was a rich, weathered brown, and his wrinkles carved so deep they looked like he'd been born with them. His blue eyes were clear, though—sharp enough to make me feel like a kid caught sneaking out after bedtime.

"Mr. Vincent," Jet said, hands lifted in a show of peace.

"You know me. Jet Rivers. Outdoor Experiences. June Spenser is my boss."

Brad squinted at him. "You run those tours up in the hills," he said.

"That's right."

He took a half step back.

"It's hot out here," Jet added, casual. "Mind if we come in?"

There was a long beat. Then Brad lowered the shotgun with a grunt that was half throat-clear, half judgment on the state of the world.

"I called Vic," he said, opening the door. "So if you're up to something, forget it."

We stepped inside. The house was clean, in that bare-minimum kind of way. No clutter. No photos. Just worn furniture and the faint scent of dust and coffee.

Kashvi didn't miss a beat.

"We want to talk about Peter Trent," she said. "And I brought these for you," she added, pulling three books from her purse.

I expected thrillers or military memoirs. Instead—*It Starts With Us, It Ends With Us*, and *Hello Beautiful*.

Brad caught my look and raised one bushy brow. "I like a good story," he said, piling the books on a side table. "And I got a lot of time to read."

Fair enough.

"You run the diner," he added, giving me a once-over. "Heard you do a decent breakfast."

I gave a shrug. He didn't seem to want an answer.

"Sit down," Brad said, waving a hand at the couch. "Ask your questions."

We'd all passed some kind of test, apparently.

I sat and waited for Kashvi to do the talking while I took notes. If Vic was on his way over, we'd need to be done before another round of suspicion showed up.

"Woody told us you were at Trent's seminar," Kashvi began. "We're trying to figure out why someone would want him dead."

Brad didn't launch into a lecture about letting the cops handle things. He just tsked. "About time someone showed those two how to do their job."

"So George Kramer came to talk to you?" I asked.

"Yesterday afternoon." Brad leaned back in his chair. "Poor guy's as lost as an elephant on Fifth Avenue."

I couldn't help it. Brad's tone implied he wasn't as disgusted with the detectives as his words sounded. "Don't you feel sorry for them?"

"A little," Brad said. "Don't know fact one about this town."

"We can pass on what you know," Jet offered. "Keep a little distance between you and the cops." Jet stood and wandered to the fridge. "Want a drink?"

"If I wanted something from my own fridge, I'd get it." Brad shot him a look. "And don't start a lecture about hydration. Vic already chewed me out this morning. I'm fine."

I fought the urge to push things along. Brad wasn't in a hurry, and if Jet and Kashvi weren't worried, I shouldn't be either.

Finally, Brad spoke again. "That Peter guy was desperate," he said, like we'd asked him a question. "Almost got me. Woody and Norma made some good points. Felt like an idiot not seeing it myself."

Kashvi nodded. "We haven't heard much about what happened after people left. Sounds like you stayed until the end."

Brad's mouth flattened. "When I told him I wasn't interested, Trent said I'd be sorry."

28

I couldn't believe Peter would have threatened an old man. "Was it a real threat?" I asked. "Maybe he meant 'you'll be sorry when everyone makes money.'"

"Not sure," Brad said. He was looking anywhere but at us, and it made me wonder if he was lying—or maybe just embarrassed he hadn't stood up to Peter.

"I just walked away," he added after a moment. "Figured I had some thinking to do and wasn't in the mood for a fight." He gave a sharp shrug. "By the time I decided to ask him what he meant, he was dead." Then he paused. "I wasn't the only one, though."

Jet leaned in. "He threatened more people? I thought con men were all charm and schmooze."

Brad made a sound, half laugh, half scoff. "That's what you'd think. But looking back... I had the feeling he was in trouble himself. Like the money wasn't for him. Like he owed it to someone who scared him."

I didn't love that theory. Something about it made my skin crawl. "Who else did he threaten?" I asked, keeping my voice steady.

Brad scratched at his chin, then leaned back. "He was talking to Alistair before we started," he said. "No one else around. They didn't see me—hard to when I was hiding beside the open door, listening in."

Jet gave him a look. "Didn't take you for the eavesdropping type."

Brad gave a short bark of a laugh that didn't quite reach his eyes. "You live long enough, you learn how to listen when it matters." He looked toward the window. "I think Alistair bought in. Regretted it. They argued. I couldn't catch much, but Alistair yelled, 'You can't talk to me like that,' and stormed off. Though that man storms everywhere."

No wonder Alistair was working overtime to point fingers my way. He knew he was a prime suspect. I made a mental note to talk to Jet and Kashvi about that later.

Kashvi pulled us back on track. "Do you think the detectives suspect you?"

She kept her tone neutral, but I could tell she was nudging us back to our actual list of questions.

"Neither of them asked," Brad said, rubbing his hands together like he was trying to warm them. "But I figured it's only a matter of time before they do."

He pushed himself up out of the chair, moving slower than he had earlier. "I dug out a couple of receipts from the day Peter died," he said. "Figured they'd come asking eventually."

He disappeared down the hallway.

Jet gave me a look. "Why wouldn't they ask about an alibi?"

"Maybe it's not like TV," Kashvi answered, pulling out our list from her bag. "We could ask."

Jet nodded toward the hallway. "Let's see what he gives us first."

Brad came back with a battered envelope and a pair of folded slips. "Hunting," he announced. "License renewal and ammo. Good thing I kept them. Took the garbage to the dump the next morning." He handed them over. "Didn't bag anything that day, so no meat in the freezer to prove where I was."

The receipts were legit—dated, signed, time-stamped. I didn't see Brad as the kind of man to build an alibi and then turn around and kill someone. But then, I hadn't seen Peter Trent's murder coming either.

"Anyone else at the seminar mad enough to kill?" Jet asked. "Other than Alistair."

Brad's mouth twitched. "Who else did Woody rat on?"

The grin softened his face a little. For a second, he looked less like a suspicious recluse and more like someone's mischievous granddad.

"Emily Stonehouse and Betty Franks," Kashvi said, checking her notebook like we had so many names she couldn't keep track.

Brad nodded. "Emily was mad at everyone. If she was gonna commit murder, I figured it'd be Woody or Norma for ruining her dream."

"And Betty?" Jet asked.

Brad exhaled slowly. "Disappointed. Not mad."

It was useful. We were heading to Emily next. Or we had planned to—until Brad dragged things out.

Kashvi pushed a little harder. "We've got three more names. Who do you remember being there?"

Brad gave her a sidelong look. "Who do you have?"

He was playing games. I was sure of it now. And if Vic showed up, we might have more trouble than we needed.

Neither Jet nor Kashvi seemed concerned, though. Maybe I was still too new at this.

Kashvi smiled wide. "You've given us some good details. But you're not the only one sharing names. We already know Alistair was there. June Gordon. Katie Wise." She let that hang for a second, then added, "Norma and Woody aren't the only people feeding us information. Don't you want to be the first with something new?"

Appeal to his competitive streak. Smart move.

"There's a name missing," Brad said slowly.

Before he could tell us who, the front door banged open.

"Brad?" a voice called.

Vic.

I felt the mood shift in the room like a drop in air pressure.

Brad's jaw clenched. "Front room," he called back.

And just like that, we were out of time.

nyone seeing them together wouldn't doubt they were related. Those eyes—bright, cutting blue— had a way of looking straight through you.

Brad's were softened by age and a lifetime of crustiness. Vic's? Not so much. He was six feet of lean muscle, the kind of build that said fireman without anyone having to tell you. Where Brad was stocky, Vic was all clean lines and quiet control.

The contrast hit me harder than I expected.

"Hey, Vic," Brad said, waving him in like we were old friends and not someone he'd called for help with. "False alarm. Grab a beer and join us."

Kashvi nudged me with her elbow, and I blinked back to attention. "Fireman," she murmured, confirming my guess. "We'll talk later."

I wasn't sure if she meant about Vic or my reaction to him. Either way, I gave her a look that was supposed to say don't start. It probably didn't work.

I cleared my throat. "We were just leaving."

Vic ignored that and stepped into the room, cold beer in hand, like he owned the place. "What are you here for?" He took a pull from the bottle, watching us over the top. "Not like you've visited before."

So the grouchiness was hereditary.

I kept my expression neutral.

"It's about that murder," Brad said. "And I get visitors. Don't get to thinking you know everything about me."

Jet filled Vic in on the basics, leaving out any details that might make us look like we were running an amateur investigation. We'd danced that line enough.

Vic shook his head when Jet finished. "Bad idea," he said. "You need to tell the cops and let them follow up."

It wasn't the first time we'd heard that advice. And since neither Kashvi nor Jet jumped in, I did.

"We've passed on what we have," I said. "Not gossip—facts. But you know this town better than I do. How sure are you that people will tell Detectives Kramer and Collett everything?"

Vic tipped his head slightly, considering me.

I could feel the weight of his stare. It wasn't flirtatious, exactly. More like he was taking a measure.

I forced myself to meet his gaze. No way was I going to be the one to blink.

After a long drink from his bottle, he shrugged. "You've got a point." He set the beer down carefully on the table. "I told the sheriff it was a mistake bringing in outsiders. Didn't have much of a choice, though. Not after the scandal."

I filed that away because there was something behind his words.

"What's stopping me from passing this along?" Vic asked suddenly. His gaze was still on me.

I raised a brow. "Who would you tell?"

Brad jumped in before Vic could answer. "You and George Kramer don't exactly get along," he said. "That thing with the arson investigation?" The disgust in his voice was clear.

Vic didn't rise to it. He just sighed. "I could go to the sheriff."

Brad bristled. "I never thought anyone in my family would end up a snitch. Ashamed of you."

He shoved himself out of his chair but didn't stand fully. Posturing, mostly. I hoped.

I stepped in quickly. "What arson?"

Vic's expression didn't shift much, but he answered. "Investigation," he said flatly. "Brad likes to make it sound dramatic. Kramer and I disagreed over jurisdiction. I won. He didn't like it."

"You're an arson investigator?" I wasn't sure why that surprised me. Maybe because this conversation was rapidly becoming all about fires.

"Just a fireman," Vic corrected. "We don't have enough incidents to justify a separate investigator."

I'd thought the whole rivalry between firefighters and cops was mostly TV nonsense. Apparently not.

"So you think poking into this investigation is going to make things better?" Brad said, fixing Vic with a look. "Or are you just trying to get even?"

Vic let out a long breath. "It shouldn't matter. This is a murder case. Egos shouldn't get in the way."

"But they already have," I said. "And if you take what we've found and go over George's head, he's going to see it as personal. Whether it is or not."

Vic studied me again, like he was recalculating. Then he stood, draining the last of his beer. "Fine. You're all adults. I just hope you don't get my uncle dragged into something dangerous."

Brad was on his feet in a flash, grabbing the shotgun from where it leaned against his chair. "Don't you say I'm fragile, boy."

"I was going to say stubborn," Vic said, rolling his eyes. "Put that down. It's not loaded."

Brad gave him a hard stare before returning the shotgun to its place. "You'd wrap me in cotton if you had your way," he muttered. "Just because we're the only family left here doesn't mean you get to make my choices."

I caught the faint thread of pride under Brad's grumbling. It was hard to tell whether Vic heard it too.

"I've got to get to work," Vic said, heading for the door.

We all watched him leave. When the door shut behind him, Brad exhaled like he'd been holding his breath.

"That boy," he said, shaking his head. "Thinks he's the only one who knows how to handle a fire."

Kashvi stood. "We should go too. We've got Betty and Emily to talk to before it gets too late."

It wasn't even four o'clock, but I took the hint. She wanted out of here before Vic came back or Brad picked up the shotgun again.

As we gathered our things, Jet spoke up. "You mentioned someone else was at the seminar? Before Vic arrived."

Brad nodded. "I'm surprised no one mentioned her. But I guess it depends how you asked." He scratched his chin. "Some folks are real literal, so they wouldn't think about her. Marilee Green. She set up the room for the meeting, but she wasn't there for his nonsense."

Kashvi made a quick note. "Did she do anything that might make her a suspect?"

Brad frowned. "Trent didn't exactly thank her for her

work. She left before the meeting broke up. Don't know if she came back after. Could've been to finish cleanup. Could've been something else."

He shrugged like it didn't matter.

But I got the feeling Brad didn't say things unless they did.

30

I couldn't shake a flicker of satisfaction that we had another lead. It felt wrong to be happy—considering we were chasing a killer—but I was starting to understand that news in this town came with a whole range of emotions.

There was a murder in Nueva Vida, but secrets—small ones, big ones, and everything in between—seemed to be just another part of life here. Brad's offhand mention of Vic and George's feud was a reminder that small towns held grudges as easily as they handed out second chances.

There were a dozen ways to carve out a place in a new community. Mine, so far, had been to stay patient and not get involved. George's approach seemed to be staking out his territory and making sure people knew it. Neither one of us was exactly winning hearts and minds.

"We should update the murder board," Kashvi said as Jet finally hit smoother pavement. The road out to Brad's was not designed for thinking, let alone conversation.

"Two more interviews," I said, my head already pounding at the thought. "If we keep running back to town every time we find something new, we'll be at this until winter."

Running a diner and investigating a murder was draining me dry. I wasn't sure whether it was lack of sleep or sheer stress, but something had to give. Soon.

"We'll head to Emily's first," Jet said, glancing at me in the rearview mirror. There was something in his expression —maybe mischief. "You were smitten, Eliza."

I rolled my eyes. "No point denying it?" The way he and Kashvi looked at me told me the answer. "I was expecting someone completely different," I said. "You could've warned me."

Kashvi giggled and poked Jet's arm. "We wanted to see your reaction. Maybe your ideal man in uniform isn't a detective after all."

"Stop trying to set me up," I said—but ruined it by laughing. "I'm not ready. Just because I appreciate a good-looking man doesn't mean I need one in my life."

"It's not up to me," Kashvi said, lifting her hands in surrender. "Now you've met both prospects, nature will take its course."

I didn't bother arguing. It wasn't worth the effort. Kashvi's love of romance novels convinced her that everyone had a soulmate waiting in the wings.

My own history had taught me otherwise.

Besides, if those were my choices—broody cop or arrogant fireman—I was probably better off single.

EMILY STONEHOUSE'S home was a neat rancher, just two streets over from Norma's.

She answered the door like she was expecting an interview from Town & Country magazine.

A silk scarf—real silk, if I had to guess—was tied just so against her crisp knit top. Her camel-colored skirt was the exact right length, and the pearls in her ears gleamed like they got polished every morning. Not exactly the image I had for someone who was constantly getting into dubious money-making schemes.

She poured tea into fine china cups and passed around a plate of perfectly arranged cookies.

"What can I do to help you?" she asked.

"We're trying to assist the police in solving the murder," Kashvi said, explaining our involvement in her usual calm, efficient way.

I paid less attention to the words and more to Emily's reaction. Which was to say—there wasn't one. Not a flicker of surprise or discomfort. Just a smooth nod, as if she'd been expecting us.

"The police already have my statement," Emily said. "I didn't hold anything back. Unlike some people we both know."

Judgy much? Although, in this case, she wasn't wrong.

Kashvi pressed on. "Can I ask why you attended the seminar? It seems a little... speculative for you."

Emily smoothed her skirt—no wrinkles, of course— then took a delicate sip of tea. "I suspected it was a con," she said. "You know I used to sell products. Mostly legitimate— Avon, things like that—but a few turned out to be... less ethical. I stopped as soon as I realized, but I recognize the patterns now. I wanted to make sure no one else fell victim."

That wasn't exactly how Woody had told it. If I remembered correctly, he'd said Emily was the most interested of the lot.

"I recognized all the hallmarks of a confidence game," Emily continued, her tone just a little too smooth. "Too good to be true, exclusivity, the 'inside track.' It wasn't subtle, not if you've seen it before."

Jet smiled faintly. "I don't know if I'd catch on as fast."

Emily gave him a look. "You would. You're not gullible."

There wasn't much more to dig out.

Emily seemed like the type who, if she had anything else to say, would have already given it to the police—on official letterhead and notarized.

Kashvi closed her notebook with a soft snap. "Do you have any idea who might've killed Peter Trent?"

Emily's expression didn't change. "That man was awful. Everyone there probably wanted to kill him. But no—I don't have any idea who actually did. There wasn't much of a motive. No one gave him money, did they? So why kill him?"

BETTY FRANKS LIVED on the far side of town, in one of the cottages attached to a tidy retirement home. The building was cheerful enough, but after I met her, I couldn't help thinking that Betty was someone who would prefer a little more chaos in her life.

She met us in the dining room, waving us toward a table like we were old friends coming for coffee.

"That man was a bully," she said, no preamble. "Exceedingly rude. I don't know how he convinced me it was legitimate. I was reaching for my checkbook before Woody and Norma set me straight. I must be getting old."

She didn't look frail to me—probably well into her eighties, but sharp-eyed and still fast with a zinger if you gave her half a chance.

"Con men are good at what they do," Jet said gently. He patted her hand like a favorite grandson. "At least you've got friends looking out for you."

Betty sighed. "I was hoping to buy my granddaughter a bigger place. One with a separate suite. So I could be with family again." She gave us a faint smile. "They visit all the time, don't get me wrong. But this place is full of old people. I need more stimulation. That's probably why I'm losing my mind."

"I don't think you're losing anything," Kashvi said.

Betty grinned. No new information, but a healthy dose of honesty. She agreed with everything we'd already heard, nodded along to the gossip, and confirmed Trent was a menace.

A small clutch of women came into the room, knitting bags over their arms.

"My knitting club," Betty said, pushing back her chair. "Go on and show that new detective how to do his job." She winked. "Good luck."

31

J et dropped me off at EB Eats so I could grab dinner for the three of us.

Jacquie was already wiping down the counter and stacking menus for tomorrow's opening. She handed me a paper bag filled with tuna melts, fries, and a wink. "I'll open again in the morning," she said before I could ask. "No sense waiting until noon."

"I owe you, Jacquie."

"Yes, you do," she replied, smiling. "But that's what makes it fun."

By the time I got back to the bookstore, Kashvi was waiting at the door like I was delivering treasure instead of sandwiches.

"Smells great. Come on, quick—let me lock up."

She barely gave me enough space to step inside before turning the bolt with a decisive click.

"Okay... what's the rush?" I asked, heading for the table where Jet had already laid out sodas from her small fridge.

He stood in front of the murder board, hands on his

hips, like a detective from an old TV show trying to will the evidence to reveal secrets.

Kashvi's eyes gleamed. "We've got an idea. Maybe we already know enough. One of the names on that board is either the killer—or knows who it is."

I wasn't convinced. We'd collected plenty of names, and maybe two real suspects, but everything still felt loose. Threads, not knots. Kashvi had a spool of red yarn on the table, and I heard the printer click out another page at the cash desk. She was on a roll, and I didn't have the heart to put a damper on her optimism.

I unpacked the sandwiches and fries, laying out napkins like makeshift plates. "Let's eat while it's hot. We can play detective after."

They joined me at the table, still scribbling notes even as they dug into their food.

"Two more people," Jet said between bites. "Marilee Green and Alistair."

"Alistair," I muttered. "If he's the killer, that'll be one less person screaming at me about EB Eats."

Jet grinned and didn't argue.

"Tell me about Marilee," I said. "I don't know her at all."

Kashvi pushed her notebook aside and grabbed a fry. "She's around our age. Runs a publicity company and calls herself an event planner. Lately, she's trying to become an influencer, but there's not a lot to work with around here."

"Side hustle," Jet added. "She started offering event planning on her website maybe six months ago. My guess? Business isn't exactly booming."

I picked up my sandwich but didn't take a bite yet. PR and event planning were good reasons for her to have worked with Pete. But walking out before the seminar ended? That didn't scream professional.

"Do we have time to meet with her in the morning?" I asked. "Jacquie's already covering me, but I don't want to leave her alone all day."

"I checked Marilee's online calendar," Jet said. "Wide open. I booked us for eight."

"And Alistair?" I glanced at them both. "Do we really want to poke that bear?"

Jet sighed. "I'll do it. After we talk to Marilee. You two wait outside Dunes. I'll order a beer and see if he says anything useful."

The relief that washed over me was probably more obvious than I wanted. Alistair and I might not really be rivals, but he acted like we were, and I didn't need to get dragged into another of his imaginary feuds.

"We'll play it by ear," Kashvi said, scribbling a note on our action list. "Let's focus on Marilee first."

I nodded. "As long as you two are good for the morning?"

"Mallory's covering the store until noon," Kashvi said. "I'm free until then."

"June's in the office tomorrow," Jet said. "She won't miss me till after lunch."

Kashvi crumpled her napkin and stood. "Let's get this on the board."

The printer had spit out a new photo—Marilee's. I helped Kashvi pin it up next to Peter's, replacing the question mark. The resolution wasn't great, probably pulled from her website.

She stood leaning against a brick wall, curly bob a little too perfect, blue eyes aimed at the camera with an expression that might've been mysterious but came across more like 'I know something you don't, and I'm going to use it against you'.

"She gives me mean girl vibes," Kashvi said, stepping back to examine the layout. "Nice enough until you've got something she wants."

"She's always been friendly with me," Jet said.

Kashvi rolled her eyes. "She's different with women."

Jet held up his hands in mock surrender. "Okay. Point taken."

I stared at the board. "Is she really a suspect? I mean, Marilee Green doesn't scream murderer."

"Maybe she confronted him, and it got out of hand," Kashvi said. "We should prepare for the interview like she is a suspect, just in case."

I looked at our updated action list. Interviews and nothing but interviews. No motel, no crime scene, nothing that would push George or Denise over the edge if they found out. Small mercies.

Marilee's name was bolded and underlined in Kashvi's neat handwriting. Alistair, June Gordon, and Katie Wise followed in smaller letters.

"What about these two?" I asked, pointing at June and Katie.

"We'll get to them," Kashvi said. "But first, Marilee. Look."

She motioned for me to step back from the wall. Sometime during dinner, they'd finished connecting the yarn. Two clusters had emerged—one centered on Peter Trent. The other on Marilee Green. A single red string linked them.

"I guess that makes her a suspect," I said.

No one argued.

32

We ended the night agreeing to meet at the bookstore by seven.

Ten minutes after I got home, Jet sent a text—Marilee had accepted the appointment at her home office.

I should have stopped drinking caffeine hours earlier. That last soda kept me wired until midnight. By then, my house was not just tidy but clean. I'd organized invoices for the diner, thought about next week's specials, and rejected a long list of murder-themed dish names my tired brain kept offering up. I finally settled on a Cuban sandwich with a twist—what the twist was, I'd figure out later.

Even after I went to bed, my mind kept spinning. Part of me was sure we were close to solving the case. Part of me wondered why I was so sure. And part of me worried about Will.

Good thing I didn't have to be up until six. After everything we'd done, today was not the day to be running on fumes.

. . .

THE BOOKSTORE WAS STILL DARK when I got there.

I stood outside, thinking. Yes, I'd spent most of the night thinking, but daylight made it feel less like worrying and more like planning. We had two suspects—Alistair and Marilee. Which meant we should be talking to George, not going off to confront anyone.

I could call Denise instead, but the thought of her barking at me drained any enthusiasm I had for that.

"Morning," Kashvi said as she arrived.

Her energy cut through my brooding. "Where's Jet?" I asked. They usually showed up together.

"Getting the van," she said, unlocking the door. "Give me a second."

I watched her through the glass as she hurried inside, turning off the alarm and flipping on the lights. A moment later, she waved me in and headed straight for the back room.

"We had a thought," she said, tossing her jacket on the back of a chair. "Our priority is Marilee, not Alistair. I don't think he'd do much more than make a scene. I don't know if George or Denise has her on their radar yet, but I'd bet someone told them about her by now. Too many people saw her at the seminar. And Alf thought Peter's partner was a woman."

I followed her into the back, thinking she'd nailed the reasons for not talking to Alistair. "So we talk to George first?"

"If we tell them what we're planning, they'll stop us," she said flatly.

Jet walked in carrying a tray with three coffees. He handed me one without a word.

"So when do we tell them?" I asked. I was hoping they'd

say after we talked to Marilee—but I wasn't holding my breath.

"We don't have enough information to accuse her of anything," Jet said.

True.

And I had personal experience with how fast an accusation could spiral.

"When I was accused of murdering Joseph, the stain of it didn't go away. Even after I was cleared. Even after they found the real killer. Some people... they just believed the worst."

"What made you call the police that night?" Kashvi asked, curious. "You said you met your source. Not a suspect."

I thought back. I was completely fooled by the killer that time. I'd gone in blind. "Maybe it was where she wanted to meet. It was a construction site, after hours. I guess something about it didn't sit right. And I figured... no one would hear me scream."

Kashvi nodded slowly. "So we don't want to do that to Marilee. What people did to you. Not the meeting in a dark, deserted location. We don't want to walk in assuming she's guilty."

"Exactly," I said. "We make a plan. We go talk to her. And just before we go in, we let George know. Give him time to get there if he wants to."

Jet sipped his coffee. "He'll probably show up in time to arrest one of us instead."

"Better that than not coming at all," I said.

It wasn't a perfect solution. But at some point, we'd hit this wall no matter what.

If we waited too long, we'd risk losing any chance to learn the truth.

"I've been thinking," I said. "Brad started our interview with a shotgun—and we didn't even think he was the killer. Now we're going to talk to a prime suspect. We need more than a list of questions. We need an exit plan."

Kashvi and Jet exchanged a look, then smiled.

"We were just saying the same thing," Kashvi said.

"We stick together," Jet added. "And we make sure we can get out fast if something feels wrong."

A flash of memory hit me—standing at that construction site, telling myself not to go in, and then ignoring my own instincts.

"Rules," I said. "And no one talks anyone into breaking them."

They both nodded.

We sat there for a minute, drinking our coffee, watching the red string on the murder board sway gently in the breeze from the overhead fan. Marilee's photo sat at the center of one cluster now, connected by a thin red line to Peter Trent.

"We're close," Kashvi said quietly.

I wasn't sure if she meant to solving the case or to crossing a line.

Either way, she was right.

33

There was no point calling for reinforcements before we got to Marilee's place. Both George and Denise had been clear—they didn't want us involved in the hunt for the killer. So, we agreed: wait until we had something real to report. Passing along solid info should avoid another lecture about wasting people's time.

By the time Jet pulled up at the curb in front of Marilee's house, the three of us had hammered out a plan. We'd go in acting like we didn't suspect her—because maybe we didn't. I liked to think of it as being thorough. Making sure we weren't jumping to conclusions. We'd treat her the same way we'd treated everyone else.

If things took a turn, one of us would step outside and call George. If Marilee wasn't the killer—despite the uneasy feeling we all shared—that only left Alistair, no matter how much we agreed he was all bluster and no follow-through.

"Call George now," Jet said, still staring at the house through the windshield.

I blinked, turning to him. We'd just agreed to wait. What had changed? I followed his gaze.

The house looked... fine. Normal, even. A small, tired-looking house in a scrappy little cluster of homes—like a subdivision that never quite caught on. The yard could've used a trim. The carport roof listed slightly to one side.

Nothing dangerous.

Just tired.

But then I saw it in light of it being her business. She sold image makeovers for a living.

Polished, curated images. This was where she met clients? Maybe she was struggling financially, but it didn't add up. The pieces didn't quite fit. And that changed everything. None of it screamed danger. But sometimes, it wasn't about what was there.

It was about what wasn't.

I trusted Jet's gut.

I dug my phone out of my bag and dialed George. Voicemail. Great. I hung up and thought fast.

"She's seen us," Kashvi said quietly. "Hurry."

I hit Denise's number next. Another voicemail. Maybe they were both out arresting the real killer right now.

Maybe.

I didn't like maybe.

Calling the station felt like the next best option. I thumbed the number I'd added to my contacts when I first got to town. The woman at reception sounded cheerful enough.

"I'll see he gets the message," she said. "Don't worry, I'm sure he'll call you right back."

I wasn't sure. And I didn't need a callback; I needed someone here. But before I could explain, she was already moving on to the next caller.

"We've done what we can," Jet said. "If we wait any

longer, Marilee's going to get suspicious. Pretend you're still on the call so she sees you hang up."

Smart.

I climbed out of the car, phone to my ear, glanced at the screen, shook my head like I was irritated, and jabbed the button to hang up.

"Wait," I said, catching up to Jet as Kashvi fell in on my other side. "What exactly did I miss?"

Jet's jaw tightened as he glanced back toward the house. "We're a long way out, and I've got a feeling," he said. "The way she's watching us—it's not right. Not for someone expecting visitors. We booked through her business calendar, remember? There's no way she's meeting regular clients out here."

arilee stood at her front door, arms folded tight over her chest, one foot tapping like she was keeping time to a song only she could hear. Not exactly the picture of patience—or a helpful witness. She wore what they call athleisure these days—gray fleece hoodie, matching leggings, white trainers that stopped tapping the moment we joined her on the stone step.

"So what are you here for?" she asked, making no move to let us inside.

"Just a few questions," Kashvi said. "Unless you want your neighbors watching and filling in the blanks themselves, you might want to let us inside."

Direct. Probably the best way to handle someone like Marilee.

I watched the emotions shift across her face, quick flashes she couldn't quite contain. Annoyance first, followed by something sharper—a flush that might've been anger. Or maybe she was already imagining what kind of gossip might spread. She tried to play it cool, but the tapping foot gave her away again.

And she couldn't quite hold eye contact long enough to convince me she was in control of anything.

With a sharp exhale, she stepped aside. We filed in, Jet last, and she made sure to close the door firmly behind him. Inside, the place looked like someone had emptied their junk drawer across every flat surface. Papers everywhere, half-empty glasses, a stack of dirty dishes leaning precariously by the sink. Open-plan living didn't leave much room for hiding your bad habits.

Not that I could throw stones—my place had its chaotic moments—but at least it didn't smell like takeout boxes that should've been tossed a week ago. By the looks of things, Marilee didn't cook. Didn't tidy, either.

None of it fit.

Not with the glossy, perfect image she sold to clients.

And yet, here we were, invited to her home like it was the most natural thing in the world.

"Okay, let's get this over with," Marilee said, brushing past us toward the living room. "I'm busy. Don't expect me to play hostess. Big client, tight deadline."

Kashvi stepped farther into the room, and I followed without thinking. Marilee didn't seem to notice Jet shifting position to stand between her and the door.

Or maybe she did and didn't care.

"We got your name from a few people," Kashvi said evenly. "About the murder."

Marilee's eyes narrowed, and her mouth flattened into a thin line. "Why? I don't have anything to say about it. I left before that jerk was halfway through his scam. I just set things up. That's all I agreed to. He didn't pay me to watch him take suckers for a ride."

"You left," Kashvi repeated, ignoring the admission. "Why?"

Marilee huffed, her arms crossing again as she paced a short loop, one foot scuffing papers without seeming to notice. "He treated me like a servant. If he wanted me handing out flyers or refilling coffee, he should've paid for that. I was there for setup and teardown. Fifty bucks, nothing more." She stooped to grab a backpack from beside the couch. "Anyway, you've had your answers. I have an appointment."

Appointment? What happened to the tight deadline?

"Why did you agree to meet us here?" I asked. "If you had nothing to say, you could've said that over the phone. Or met us where you usually meet clients. And it's not here."

For a beat, she froze. Then her gaze swept the room, taking in the three of us, and something changed. Her shoulders tensed like a runner waiting for the starting gun.

"Get out of my house," she snapped.

And then she bolted.

She aimed for the back door, but a loose pile of papers slid under her foot, sending her sprawling hard before any of us could stop her. She hit the ground with a thud that made me wince.

"Easy," Kashvi said, already moving to help. "Come on, sit down and catch your breath."

She nodded for Jet to lift Marilee by the elbow, steadying her onto the couch. The backpack thumped down between Marilee's feet. Kashvi knelt in front of her, giving her a quick once-over.

"No sign of a concussion. Lucky. But you should really think about cleaning this place up—it's an accident waiting to happen."

Marilee glared at her, jaw tight. "I need the chaos to be

creative," she bit out. "I didn't fall because of anything I did. If you weren't cornering me, I wouldn't have run. Or do you think I make a habit of sprinting for the back door?"

"You ran because we asked a couple of questions?" I asked before I could stop myself. "That doesn't make a lot of sense."

"There are three of you," she muttered, gaze flicking over us. "How was I supposed to know you wouldn't hurt me?"

I could almost buy it.

Almost.

But Kashvi and I together weren't exactly an intimidating duo. And Jet had been nowhere near her when she took off. No, something was eating at Marilee.

Whether it was guilt or fear, I wasn't sure.

But if I had to bet, I'd lay money on it having to do with Peter's death.

35

W e sat in silence.

Kashvi next to Marilee on the couch, Jet and I across from them, close enough to block any sudden moves. I ran questions through my head, trying to find a way to crack Marilee's calm—or what was left of it.

She stared at the floor, shoulders hunched. Was she working on an excuse? A lie? Plotting her escape?

I glanced at Jet. His jaw was tight, eyes locked on her, watching for the first sign she might bolt again.

And where the heck was George?

If he was going to give us grief about playing amateur detective, the least he could do was show up to arrest the person we'd cornered for him. I checked my phone. No missed calls. No texts. Only five minutes since I'd reached out, but it felt like hours.

Maybe George was waiting on us to get the ball rolling. Maybe we needed to hand him the confession on a silver platter.

I leaned toward Jet and whispered, "Record this."

He pulled out his phone and tapped the voice recorder.

"We might not get it," he whispered back. "And I can't call for help if I'm recording. Unless you want me to put 911 on speaker."

I considered it. Marilee was shaken, but fear could make people unpredictable. Scared enough to confess? Maybe. Scared enough to lash out? Also maybe.

Before I could answer, Marilee spoke.

"I can hear you," she said, still staring at the floor. Her voice was flat. "Why are you calling the cops?"

"To take over," I said. "You hated him. You knew he was running a con. You ran before we asked a single question."

I didn't add more. I was happy to let her sit in the silence, fill in her own blanks. I gave Jet a quick shake of my head, hoping he understood.

Not yet.

Let's not push.

Kashvi shifted, crossing one leg over the other like we were chatting over coffee. "It's awful when men don't give us credit," she said, calm and conversational. "I get so mad sometimes, I have to go hide in the back room of my shop. Peter didn't think you were capable of much, did he?"

I fought to keep my face neutral. Kashvi was brilliant at this—making her voice just soft enough to sound understanding, just sharp enough to sound true.

I'd seen her handle arrogant tourists in the bookstore— starting polite, then getting firmer, then closing the door behind them. But this wasn't about getting Marilee to leave. It was about getting her to stay. And talk.

Marilee's face crumpled. "He didn't even pay me," she said, her voice cracking into a sob. "I should've said no when he offered the money. I can't afford to turn down any paying gig. I have bills. I'm trying to get my PR company off the ground."

It might have been an act. But if it was, it deserved an award. Her cheeks burned red, tears streaking down like she couldn't hold them back.

Starting a business was hard. A PR business here in Nueva Vida? I could only imagine.

"Maybe the police can tell you how to get the money from his estate," Kashvi said, as if Marilee wasn't sitting there about to confess to murder.

Calm. Gentle. I almost forgot what we were doing for half a second.

Marilee blinked up at her. "You think so? My new revenue stream's still... it's still in its infancy. Did I tell you about it?"

Kashvi shook her head. "Not yet. Why don't you start with what happened that day?"

Marilee hesitated. Her hand tightened on the backpack between her feet, knuckles white. Then she let out a shaky breath. "He called me after I left. Yelled at me. Said I should get back and clean up. I guess the event didn't go the way he wanted." She swallowed hard. "I told him not to invite Woody and Norma. They're suspicious of everything. They would've smelled the scam before it even started."

I exchanged a glance with Jet. Was she getting a cut? Was that why she stayed quiet about what Peter was doing?

"He said I should stick to my own business," Marilee continued, her voice thin. "Said he knew what he was doing." She blinked hard, as if trying to clear the memory. "When I went back, he was furious. Came at me, screaming. He grabbed my arm." Her gaze flickered over to Jet and then back to the floor. "I pushed him. He stumbled. It was fast. Too fast."

She finally looked up at us. "I didn't mean for it to happen. It was an accident."

Kashvi's tone hardened as she asked, "Then why didn't you call the police?"

Good thing she was doing the talking. I'd be asking how she accidentally stabbed him to death.

Marilee's face closed off again, mouth tight. "Those new detectives? They'd never believe me. They've been on my case since they got here."

I frowned. That didn't track. George and Denise hadn't said anything about Marilee. Their focus had been else-where—mostly on phantom gang activity.

Kashvi edged slightly away, giving Marilee space but staying on the couch. "So you left him there? In the alley?"

"He deserved it," Marilee muttered. The bitter twist to her lips said she meant it.

I let out a slow breath. "You tossed the knife into Alistair's trash bins," I said quietly. "On purpose?"

Her mouth twitched. Not a smile, but close. "Another jerk," she said. "It almost worked, didn't it?"

We had her confession. I didn't want to be here any longer than necessary. Normal life was waiting for me—well, normal-ish.

Jet could tie her up. I'd call George. Simple.

"Jet," I said, stepping toward my bag. "Secure her. I'll get George on the line."

I was pulling up George's contact when I heard the thump.

Then Jet's curse.

I spun around.

Marilee was gone.

Jet was untangling himself from Kashvi, both of them struggling to get to their feet. The backpack was missing.

And the back door stood wide open.

36

I sprinted for the back door, but I was too late. Marilee's car was already at the corner, turning right and disappearing down the street.

"What happened?" I asked, reaching to untangle Kashvi and Jet where they'd landed in a heap.

"She headbutted Jet," Kashvi said, rubbing her shoulder. "Knocked him right onto me. I think she planned it so she could keep both of us from grabbing her."

Jet hauled himself up, then helped Kashvi to her feet. "I should've been more careful," he said, grimacing. "I should've made sure Kashvi was clear before I tried to restrain her."

"It's not your fault," I said quickly. "We all missed it. She played us." I glanced at the back door again, frustration tightening my chest. "I knew something was off. The way she gave us what we wanted—it was too easy."

Jet blew out a breath, rubbing the spot on his forehead where Marilee's skull had made contact. "What now?"

"We let the police handle it," I said, forcing myself to sound practical, even though my gut twisted at the thought of standing down. "We've got the recording. George can't argue we got in the way. I'll call him again."

"I feel like an idiot," Jet muttered.

"We're not cops," I reminded him. "We're not supposed to be good at this." Even if we were getting dangerously close. "She knew exactly what she was doing."

"I might—" Kashvi started.

Jet's attention snapped back to her, concern sharpening his features. "Are you hurt?"

"I'm fine." Kashvi held out a hand to keep him at bay, irritation flashing across her face. "Nothing broken. Probably not even bruised. And will you let me finish?"

Jet opened his mouth, but I shot him a look. We both fell silent, giving Kashvi the floor.

"Thank you," she said dryly. "I slipped my phone into her backpack when I helped her onto the couch."

It took me a beat.

Then it clicked. "We can track her."

Jet let out a breath that was half a laugh and hugged her hard before digging out his car keys. "Let's go before we lose her."

"Wait," I said, holding up a hand. "Can you actually track her? I don't want to get halfway out there and lose the signal."

Kashvi nodded. "I gave you both access when we went to that folk festival, remember?"

I checked my phone. Sure enough, Kashvi's phone was on the move, a pulsing dot heading out toward the hills beyond town.

Jet was already scanning his own screen. "She's past Woody's place. My phone's nearly dead, though. Recording drained it." He frowned. "I'll have to charge it while we drive."

And if we lost her now, we might not get another chance. Marilee could be long gone before George and Denise got anywhere close.

"New plan," I said, thinking fast. "Jet, you stay here. Plug in and get your phone charged, there's a cord on the counter. You can send George the recording and fill him in on everything."

"And you?" Jet's voice dropped dangerously low, his gaze snapping to mine.

"Kashvi and I will follow Marilee," I said before he could argue. "We'll track her phone. I'm sharing my location now —you can track me, too."

I tapped the option and sent the invite. "Two trackers are better than one."

Jet stared at me like he was ready to deliver a full lecture on why this was the worst idea in history. But time was bleeding away, and Marilee was getting farther ahead with every second we stood there.

"It's the best option," I pressed. "We can't stall. We'll be careful."

He looked at Kashvi.

She nodded, already plugging his phone into the charger on the kitchen counter.

"We'll be careful," she echoed. "And we won't confront her."

For a long second, he didn't move. Then he sighed and handed Kashvi the keys. "Fine. Don't get hurt. And Eliza?"

"Yeah?"

"Don't make me regret trusting you both."

I gave him a small, tight smile. "We won't."

Kashvi had the car started by the time I finished my call to George. He actually picked up this time.

"You need to meet Jet at Marilee Green's house," I told

him. "He's got everything you need. The confession. The recording."

"Where are you?"

Typical George. No thank you, just more questions.

"Jet will tell you everything," I said, hanging up before he could argue.

I slid into the passenger seat as Kashvi pulled out onto the street, my phone already open to the map. The dot marking Marilee's device was slowing down.

"She's not moving as fast now," I said.

"Speeding wouldn't help," Kashvi murmured. "Not with the cops already on her tail."

I nodded, but I wasn't so sure.

Marilee was desperate.

And desperate people were dangerous.

37

I spent half the drive holding onto the door handle, bracing myself against Kashvi's aggressive cornering. The van lurched like it was begging for mercy.

"I hope she's not planning to drive all day," I managed, teeth clacking as we hit another pothole. "If she gets to a highway, we'll lose her."

"She's only got the backpack and the clothes she's wearing," Kashvi said, eyes locked on the road. "I'm betting she has a place out here. A stash. Maybe even a go-bag."

The van shuddered as a gust of wind shoved it sideways.

"Why would she have a go-bag?" I asked. "It's only been a few days. She was laying low—why run now? If she waited a week, a month, no one would even question her leaving."

"Because she's not the type to stick around and explain herself," Kashvi said. "And she's done this before. I'd put money on it. People like Marilee always have an exit strategy."

I checked my phone, gripping the strap with my other hand as the van bounced again. "She turned off about half a mile ahead."

Kashvi eased up on the gas, the engine settling into a low growl. "We'll hang back. No sense letting her spot us."

I glanced at the screen again.

"She's stopped."

"Good."

Kashvi coasted the van to the side of the road, tires crunching on gravel. She killed the engine and stared ahead. "There are a few cabins farther along. If she's holed up, we've got a front-row seat."

I scanned the stretch of empty road behind us. Still no sign of George. No messages. No updates.

"I don't know how long we can wait," I said, not hiding the frustration in my voice. "George still hasn't updated me."

"Text Jet," Kashvi said, eyes still fixed on the narrow dirt driveway ahead. "He'll know something."

I sent the text. Nothing. Not even a read receipt. A knot twisted in my stomach.

"His phone's charging," Kashvi reminded me. "Or tracking us. Either way, he's doing his job. We do ours."

I envied her calm. All I had was a tight throat and too many memories of walking into situations I wasn't qualified for. This wasn't how I pictured things going when I signed up to feed people with diner food.

"We should take a look," Kashvi said, cracking her door open.

A dry, dusty wind swirled in, carrying the scent of sunbaked dirt and pine.

"No," I blurted, reaching for her arm and missing by inches. "It's too dangerous."

"We won't go far." She stepped out, boots crunching softly on the gravel. "Just a peek through the window. She won't be standing there waiting for us."

"We promised Jet," I said, but I was already shifting toward the door. I wasn't letting Kashvi go alone.

She glanced back at me, her expression softening just a fraction. "I know."

I climbed out and shut the door quietly behind me, scanning the trees, the road, the empty world around us. "We can't stay here all day," I muttered.

"Nope," Kashvi agreed. "And we can't let her get away again."

I blew out a shaky breath. "Okay. But we're careful."

"Always." She grinned, but her eyes stayed serious.

We started toward the cabin, moving low and quiet. The wind carried the smell of dust and old pine needles. No birdsong. No voices.

Just the sound of our steps crunching the dirt as we crept closer to Marilee's hideout.

38

S neaking up to the window was no problem. No nosy neighbors. No joggers. No dog walkers. This wasn't a neighborhood with casual witnesses and safety in numbers. It was isolation. I'd be surprised if any of the other scattered cabins out here were occupied—besides the one Marilee was holed up in.

Cabin was generous. It was a truck camper, rusted and slumped on flat tires, long past its prime. Probably dragged out here years ago and left to rot.

If you came to fish or hunt, maybe it was enough. But the rust had eaten deep into the siding, and I'd bet it wasn't far from breaking through to the interior.

Someone had backed it into the lot sideways—hitch end facing toward the left, driver long gone. The side facing us, the street side, had a couple of grimy windows and a door that looked like it had rusted itself shut a decade ago. Solid. Unmoving. No one was getting in or out through there anymore.

The windows were high up—too high for us to see through without a ladder. I crouched anyway. Habit.

Marilee wouldn't be able to see us for the same reason we couldn't see her. I pointed toward the back of the camper, and Kashvi nodded, motioning that she'd check the far side.

She circled around the front, retracing our steps to stay out of view of any potential sightlines. I waited, scanning the area.

No movement. No sounds but the wind in the trees. A moment later, Kashvi reappeared. She gave me a thumbs-up and an encouraging smile.

No other exits on the far side. That left the back.

We moved together, circling carefully to the rear of the camper. And there it was. Someone had cut a new door into the center of the back wall—rough, unfinished, with daylight leaking in through the gaps.

It looked like it had been done fast, maybe desperate, maybe years ago. Either way, it was the only functional entrance now. And it faced the back of the lot, away from the road and any casual passerby. I didn't want to think about what had crawled through that gap. Mosquitoes. Spiders. Worse.

From inside, we could hear thumps, things being tossed around. In the two minutes she'd been here, she could've grabbed a go-bag and bolted. But by the sound of it, she was still hunting for something.

She hadn't planned this far ahead. Our arrival at her house must've been the trigger that set her running.

Kashvi pressed her back to the wall, beside the new door. She caught my eye and mouthed something. Remember our promise, I thought.

I exhaled slowly. We were supposed to stay safe. Wait for George. But if Marilee made a break for it, we couldn't let her slip away again.

I tilted my head toward the door and raised my eyebrows in a question. Go in? Wait her out?

Then there was a solid thud inside.

A curse.

And then, clear as anything: "Finally."

I tensed. Whatever she'd been looking for, she'd found it.

39

I shoved the door to close it tight and leaned against it, bracing with everything I had. Kashvi joined me, shoulder to shoulder, both of us pressing into the rough metal. We were keeping our promise. Staying safe. As long as Marilee didn't manage to get the door open, we were in the clear.

I grabbed my phone one-handed and sent a quick text to George and Jet: Where are you?

Then Kashvi elbowed me and said, "Oh no."

Inside, we heard the thudding sounds—sharp and repetitive. Kicks.

"She's going after a window," Kashvi said.

"She won't fit through," I said, though doubt tugged at me.

The windows were six feet up, narrow. But desperation made people do the impossible. My phone pinged with a reply, but I didn't have time to check it.

"I'm going to see what she's doing," I told Kashvi. "Hold the door, in case this is a trick."

Kashvi nodded, digging her heels in harder like she was a human doorstop.

I sprinted around the camper, cursing at my phone for not unlocking fast enough. As I reached the side, an entire window frame popped out and hit the dirt near my feet with a thud. Rust flakes puffed up in clouds.

A moment later, Marilee's head appeared—wild-eyed and red-faced, her breathing ragged.

"Don't make this worse," I shouted. "Wait for the police."

"I'm not caught yet," she barked back, yanking her head inside.

I ran back to Kashvi.

"She's trying to squeeze through. We need—"

A heavy thud cut me off.

Something hit the ground on the far side of the camper, followed by the screech of metal.

"How secure is the original door?" I asked, panting.

"It was stuck solid. Plate over the keyhole," Kashvi said.

Another clatter. Then the unmistakable wail of tearing metal.

"Go see what she's throwing out," I said. "I'll hold the back."

Kashvi took off, and I shifted to watch the door.

But then I heard her yell. "She's coming out the window!"

I sprinted toward the side of the camper as Marilee scrambled out of the gap where the window used to be. She'd kicked out the entire frame.

She scraped her legs on the rusted edges, tearing a hole in her leggings, but she didn't care. She dropped to the ground hard, scrambled up, and made a break for it.

She was running straight for her car.

I lunged forward and grabbed at her jacket.

She wrenched herself free, leaving me holding empty sleeves.

She didn't even hesitate, pumping her arms as she sprinted toward the vehicle parked at the edge of the lot.

A car screeched into the driveway, tires spitting gravel.

Marilee skidded to a halt, cursed, and pivoted on her heel.

George's car blocked hers in, and he and Denise were already out and running toward her.

Marilee's breath hitched in frustration, and she took off in the other direction—toward the scrubby trees at the back of the lot.

George and Denise chased her without hesitation.

Jet scrambled out of the back seat and scanned the clearing. "Kashvi!" he shouted.

She was already running toward him, the backpack slung over her shoulder. It looked heavier than before, and she was struggling to keep her balance.

I jogged to meet them as shouting echoed from the trees.

Then, a scream.

A few minutes later, Denise emerged, leading a scraped-up and furious Marilee by the arm. George followed, looking like he'd wrestled a mountain lion. His suit was a wreck—dusty, covered with twigs as if someone had dropped a tin of wooden cupcake sprinkles over his head, and peppered with burrs.

A bright scratch ran down one cheek. He made his way toward us, wiping his face with his sleeve.

"I told you to stay out of this," he said, still winded.

"You're welcome," I shot back. "For doing your job."

I shoved the backpack toward him.

"Her go-bag. Kashvi's phone's inside. We'd like it back. And Jet already gave you the confession."

I wasn't sure where all the bravado came from. Adrenaline, probably. Or maybe it was the rush of knowing Marilee wasn't going to hurt anyone else.

George gave me a long, flat look. Then he nodded. "We'll process the evidence and file charges against Ms. Green."

He glanced around. "Anyone hurt?"

"We're fine," Kashvi said. "Though I'm a little disappointed we can't add assault to her list of charges."

I was thankful we weren't attacked.

"Go home," George said. "I'll contact you later."

He turned away, heading back to Marilee and Denise at the car.

"We all have work to do," I muttered after him. Then immediately regretted it. I sounded like a five-year-old arguing 'you're not the boss of me'.

But I meant it. We did have work to do.

And for once, it didn't involve chasing murderers.

40

The next morning, I was wiping down the counters after the breakfast rush. I'd closed the diner last night and then slept for nine hours straight. Turns out chasing a murderer burns a lot of energy.

The door chime rang.

"Take any seat you like," I called, not bothering to look up.

"I need to talk to you."

George. But surprisingly, he didn't sound angry. More tired than anything. Did I want to talk to him? Not really. But he was here. Might as well get it over with.

Jacquie called out an order, and Will slid past me to grab it from the pass.

Anthone gave me a look as he plucked the cloth out of my hand.

"I'll finish up here. Bring him some coffee."

"Thanks," I murmured. I turned to face George, staying on my side of the counter.

You know—for his safety. Just in case. "Marilee in jail?" I asked.

"Charged and denied bail," George said, accepting the mug of coffee Anthone handed him.

He dumped in what looked like half the sugar jar.

"And we're all going to have to testify?" I pressed.

"Probably. She's lawyered up. Ranted about how unfair life is." He took a long gulp. "But the recording you got? Closed it. You were right. She'd have been long gone if you hadn't acted when you did."

"You're welcome," I said, letting it sit there for a beat.

"That doesn't mean you can get in the way of every investigation."

I raised a brow. "Get in the way? We solved it."

George sighed, like the weight of the entire county was on his shoulders. "Fine. Helping. You helped."

He cleared his throat. "And I'm on my way to apologize to Jet and Kashvi. After this."

"You should." I poured him a refill before he could push the mug my way again.

"Thanks." He managed a ghost of a smile. "If you don't want to keep stepping into these situations, maybe tell people to start talking to us. It's hard to do the job if we're pariahs."

I met his gaze. "They talk to us because we listen. If you want people to talk to you, you need to show them you're on their side."

He sighed again. "We're trying. But it's not easy when people don't trust you."

"You've got to earn it," I said simply.

"I know," he replied. "Just... stay in your lane, Eliza. I don't want to be investigating your murder."

"Dramatic," I muttered under my breath.

But part of me got it. He'd been worried. This was his version of take care of yourself.

The door chimed again.

We both glanced over as Vic strolled in wearing his fireman gear.

George gave him a nod. "Simons."

"Kramer," Vic replied, civil to each other but with no warmth on either side.

George turned back to me. "Good work," he said, quietly enough that only I could hear. Then he drained the rest of his coffee, left a few bills on the counter, and walked away.

Vic watched him go, then continued up to the counter.

"I put in an order for the station," he said.

He was all swagger in that gear, but the way he nodded and smiled at people as he passed was easy and genuine.

"It's almost ready," Jacquie called from the kitchen.

"You don't like George," I said, grabbing condiments for his order.

Vic shrugged, the movement stiff in the heavy jacket. "You know why. I don't want to get into the details."

"Fair enough."

Jacquie passed his order through the window, two paper bags of hot food. I tucked condiments inside before stapling the tops closed and handing them over.

"I was wondering if you'd like to go for coffee sometime," Vic said as he took the bags.

"I'm pretty busy," I said. Dating hadn't exactly been on my mind lately.

"Not now," he said, grinning. "Whenever you've got time. I like how you handled the murder thing. You impressed Uncle Brad, and that's not easy. It'd be nice to get to know you."

He headed out before I could think of a better answer. I watched him go.

"You know," Will said behind me, "he's a good guy. And you do drink coffee."

Before I could reply, the door swung open again.

Alistair.

He stomped in, his boots louder than necessary, and made a beeline for the counter. He scanned the menu with his usual glare, but before I could ask him if he was really going to eat here, Mrs. Brennan—sitting nearby—cleared her throat loudly.

"What?" Alistair barked.

She raised one perfectly arched brow. "You owe that young lady an apology."

Alistair turned red. "I didn't—" He sighed, as if it was physically painful. "Just because you didn't kill that Trent crook doesn't mean you aren't trouble. And when you mess up again, I'll be watching."

Mrs. Brennan coughed again.

He threw up his hands. "Fine. Thanks for not being the killer."

"Apology accepted," I said, biting back a smile.

He grunted and stomped back out the door.

Mrs. Brennan winked at me. "Some men just need a little nudge."

I glanced around the diner. It was full of regulars, talking and eating, as normal as any other morning. But things were different.

I was different.

I smiled to myself as I wiped down the counter again. Life in Nueva Vida might not be easy—but it was mine. And for once, that felt like enough.

41

For the rest of the day, I found myself smiling for no reason.

Okay, I knew exactly why. It was nice to be wanted. Maybe not romantically—though Vic had asked me to coffee—but wanted in the sense that people actually valued me here.

People trusted me. They liked me. Even Alistair's usual storming entrance into the diner couldn't dull my mood.

My get-to-know-the-community task list was long enough that I didn't have time for dating anyway. At least, that's what I told myself.

When the diner closed, I headed over to the bookstore.

Kashvi had texted, calling it a debrief meeting. George would've had kittens if he'd known. I mean, a debrief was about learning lessons and improving for next time, right? Just the words next time were enough to make me twitch.

Jet was at the door when I arrived, and he locked it behind me, double-checking that the sign was turned to Closed.

"We're in the back," he said, his usual calm sliding toward something lighter. "A little celebration."

He ushered me past the shadowed shelves and into the well-lit back room. The murder board was gone. In its place was a framed certificate that read: For Excellence in Community Safety.

"The police gave us an award?" I asked, raising my brows as Jet handed me a champagne flute.

"Are you kidding?" Kashvi asked, popping a bottle with a grin. "I'm surprised we aren't doing community service for helping them. No, this was my idea. We made a difference. We should mark the occasion."

I raised my glass. "Here's to questionable decisions that worked out."

Kashvi clinked her glass against mine. "And to not making them again. Unless it's absolutely necessary."

"Did George stop by to thank you?" I asked.

"He did," Kashvi said. "No Denise, though. I think he didn't want her ruining the apology."

"And the warning not to help in the future," Jet added. "So, basically a 'thank you, but don't ever do this again.'"

I didn't want to get involved in another murder case. Or any kind of crime. I'd make an exception for Will, and probably his friend Cassidey, if they needed help staying out of trouble. That felt more like prevention than investigation.

But it still bothered me how people refused to talk to George and Denise. Sure, some of it was their attitude, but some of it was habit, and the job didn't exactly encourage making friends. Maybe we could help change that.

"I told George to make more effort to know people here," I said. "Maybe we could help. Get the community talking to them more."

Kashvi refilled my glass with an amused glance. "You want to help George because you like him? Or do your tastes run more to firefighters these days?"

I narrowed my eyes at her. "News travels fast."

Kashvi grinned into her glass. "Jacquie called. You're going to blush every time you see either of those men."

I looked to Jet for support.

He just shrugged. But he was smiling, and the sparkle in his eye made it worse.

"I'm not dating anyone," I insisted. "I just think it's the right thing to do if we want to stay out of future investigations."

Kashvi giggled, which I chose to believe was champagne-fueled and not part of some nefarious matchmaking scheme.

"Well," she said, surveying the room, "I think we should make this a regular thing."

"What? Champagne and pastries?" I asked.

"Community safety reviews," she said with a wink. "You never know when we'll need to save the town again."

Jet groaned, but he was still smiling.

And me? I wasn't sure what to think. But sitting there, with people I trusted, I knew one thing for certain.

Life in Nueva Vida was never boring.

And I was exactly where I was supposed to be.

What's up for Eliza next? A food fair that ends in murder! Use the Qr code below to grab your copy of Death On The Menu.

If you enjoyed reading Fries Gravy Death, please consider helping other readers to find the story by leaving a review.

FREE BOOK

Use the QR code to Claim your copy of Burned by BLT when you sign up for my newsletter learn how Eliza became so determined to clear her name.

ALSO BY PRINT

For more books by Poppy Bridgeman

scan the QR code below.

ABOUT POPPY BRIDGEMAN

Hi, I'm Poppy Bridgeman, the cozy mystery alter ego of Canadian author P A Wilson. Poppy was "born" because sometimes stories need a gentler touch—with a little magic, a dash of humor, and plenty of sleuthing spirit.

As Poppy, I write the *Witch of Henbane Island* series (where witches and festivals collide with mysteries), the *EB Eats Culinary Mysteries* (a small-town diner, a determined heroine, and murder on the menu), and the *Pages & Paws Bookstore Mysteries* (a Devon bookshop, two mischievous corgis, and plenty of secrets tucked between the shelves).

When I'm not tangled in my characters' escapades, I'm happily tangled in yarn—I knit, weave, and doodle in sketchbooks between writing sessions. I also love to travel, finding inspiration for charming settings, quirky characters, and suspicious strangers wherever I go.

Home base is the Vancouver area, where I juggle writing as both Poppy and P A Wilson. Whichever name is on the cover, I'm always chasing the next story.

 X

ACKNOWLEDGMENTS

People think that the process of writing is solitary. That's not the case for me. I have help from so many people it would be hard to acknowledge everyone, but I'll give it a try.

The support and inspiration I get from my writer's groups is incalculable. The Vancouver Writers Social Group opens my mind to other ways of telling a story. The Royal City Literary Arts Society gives me the opportunity to meet and share with other writers who have more knowledge than I do. The Other 11 Months group is where I learn about getting the words on the page. And my critique group who helps me find the best parts of the story I want to tell. Thanks to all of the members of these great groups.

Last of all, but definitely a huge part of the process, my beta readers. These are the people who love stories and are willing, and more than able, to tell me if my finished story is ready for you, my readers.